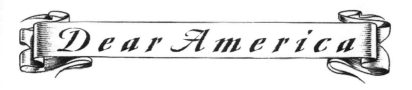

Survival in the Storm

The Dust Bowl Diary of Grace Edwards

BY KATELAN JANKE

Scholastic Inc.   New York

Dalhart, Texas
1935

Sunday, February 17, 1935

The winds are quieter than usual this afternoon. Without those sandy gusts howling across the farm, I can hear myself think. Sunday afternoons are a welcome relief from school and chores. At last I have time to sit in the hayloft and begin writing.

Helen surprised me with this diary yesterday, my twelfth birthday. The inside cover is inscribed with her neatest handwriting: *To Grace Edwards, on the occasion of your 12th birthday — Your forever friend, Helen Walker.*

Mama made a delicious birthday supper — fried chicken, mashed potatoes with cream gravy, and black-eyed peas — my favorites. She says we have to be sparing these days of how many chickens we butcher, so I savored every bite.

After supper, Mama and Daddy presented me with a beautiful book: *Anne of Green Gables.* I'd wished for it ever since Mama told me how she'd enjoyed reading it as a girl. Ruth sewed a bookmark for me out of burgundy felt with my initials embroidered in gold floss at the top. It matches the book's cover. She was very proud of her sewing accomplishment. I'm going to quit writing now, so I can begin reading the first chapter.

Monday, February 18, 1935

Ruth whined three times this evening that she wanted a diary, too, but I reminded her that I never had a diary, either, when I was seven. She began to pout — she doesn't like it when I correct her — so Mama quickly suggested we ask Daddy to tell us a story. Daddy's rendition of "Jack and the Beanstalk" perked up Ruth in no time.

Tuesday, February 19, 1935

Just as Miss Boston was fixing to dismiss school this afternoon, a norther blew in. The strong wind pushed Ruth and me from behind as we ran most of the two miles home. It felt colder than ever while I hurried through my chores. I was sure Brownie's wagging tail was going to freeze in midair as she followed me about. I couldn't even feel my toes in my shoes, and it took a good half hour to warm the feeling back into them in front of the cookstove.

Ruth came in shivering from feeding the chickens. She's still little enough to stand on the sturdy, cast-iron oven door to warm her feet. On days like this, I'm not about to bellyache over helping Mama in the warm house — the gusty winds are bad enough, but now it's bitter cold to boot!

Wednesday, February 20, 1935

This morning, Miss Boston held a ciphering contest — the fifth and sixth grades teamed against the seventh and eighth. The older pupils won again, but at least it wasn't as bad as I'd fretted it might be. I'm usually *terrible* at figuring arithmetic problems at the blackboard with everyone watching!

One thing I *am* still fretting about is Mama's never-ending dishwashing. With the wind and dust, not only do the dishes have to be washed after mealtime, but they also have to be rinsed before I can even set the table. Somehow, Mama always manages to be so particular about every plate and glass being spotless.

Yesterday's wind caused damage to pretty near everyone's winter wheat. During supper, Daddy said most of his fields now have only about half of what he planted last fall, yet for that we have to be grateful. It was comforting to hear Daddy say we're hanging on pretty well, though, compared with most others.

Daddy refilled my lamp with kerosene, so I'm going to stay awake a bit longer to read a chapter of *Anne of Green Gables*, at least until Ruth complains for me to blow out the light. When reading about Anne, it's easy to slip into her world, and I almost expect to see the green hills and rocky beaches of Prince Edward Island when I glance out the bedroom window. Instead, I see the unending treeless prairie.

Thursday, February 21, 1935

Early this morning, before Mama could call to wake us, I heard scratching on the window. Ruth heard it, too, and whispered, *"Grace!!! Someone's outside our window!"*

I tried to assure her that it wasn't anything to fret about, but truth be told, I was a bit frightened as well. Stories of house robberies and worse kept spinning through my mind.

The scratching persisted, and the wind howled eerily, like something out of a suspenseful picture show. I bravely decided to creep to the window and see who was there. When I peeked through the curtains, I saw a gigantic tumbleweed, caught up against the side of the house! It was as wide as my arms held open, and taller than my waist.

Ruth and I rushed outside for a closer look. It was by far the biggest tumbleweed imaginable, and Mama and Daddy agreed when we showed them our find. We carefully placed it in the hayloft next to our arrowhead collection, where it's quite safe from the blowing, howling wind.

Friday, February 22, 1935

I had a terrible splinter today from sweeping so long, and my finger is still sore. Used to be I'd sweep once a day — in the evening after washing the supper dishes. But with all this dust, Mama insists it now be done twice every day, in the mornings as well as the evenings.

I remember when I was younger, long before the dust always blew. I'd reach up to the peg on the wall and pull down the broom without being asked and sweep the whole house. Mama would shine with happiness and call me her "little helper." I'd be so pleased with myself, and feel proud the whole day long.

These days, it seems, I've been enlisted into Mama's army, marching into battle to fight the enemy dust. The cleaning and sweeping is a continuous cycle, and when a chore is done, I'm no longer rewarded with a big smile or approving nod. Mama grimly surveys my work, and finds any overlooked dust. On and on goes Mama's war.

Saturday, February 23, 1935

Today was a trying day. This afternoon, Mama was at the church for her Ladies Auxiliary Meeting, and Ruth and I were to get supper started. Things started out all right, but after stirring the beans for a short while, Ruth asked if she could take a break to use the privy. A good twenty minutes later I looked out the front window and saw her laughing as she played with a horned toad. She didn't seem to mind at all that I'd caught her. Instead, she showed me her "cute little horn toad." I snapped at her and marched her back into the house to finish helping, only to find the beans were burning on the cookstove, and then Ruth told me she "forgot" to go to the privy while she was outside.

When Mama returned home, I explained why the beans were burned but, as usual, Ruth only received a mild scolding for neglecting her duties.

As we sat down to supper, Ruth ran to get her cherished doll, Miss Annie. She set it on the table next to her plate and then told Miss Annie to bow her head for grace! Mama merely smiled when she saw Ruth pretending. During the rest of supper, Ruth proceeded to talk to her doll and spoon-feed it beans and cornbread. I stopped playing with my dolls long ago, and when I was *her* age, I was already busy with chores, not imaginative fancies. Ruth, and even Mama, are truly exasperating.

Sunday, February 24, 1935

I was grateful to forget about dusty chores this morning to attend church in our little schoolhouse. On Sundays, when it's a place of worship, I almost forget it's the same room where we hold school lessons. I love to hear all of the voices joined together singing hymns and praises. It sounds as if they fly through the rafters and straight into heaven.

After morning services, Daddy and a group of farmers were seriously discussing the winds that have been blowing in mighty strong gusts lately. Mr. Mayfield said he figures the wind could reduce the remaining winter wheat crop to only a third of what was planted. I glanced at the sky and wondered: How long until the clouds open up and pour out moisture like they have in the past?

For nearly four years now, wind, dust, and drought have settled over the vast Texas Panhandle. Even so, through all the turmoil, Daddy says most folks haven't yet lost hope. "Next year" the rains will come. "Next year" the ferocious winds will cease. Next year . . . but I think that deep down inside, we are all wondering the same thing: What if next year is the same?

Monday, February 25, 1935

Pastor Benson's wife told Mama about a lady who has six children and can't sew. Feeling it her duty to lend a hand, Mama stopped by the lady's house and picked up several torn dresses and shirts. Although I know it's only right to help the less fortunate, I would do almost anything to avoid sitting in a chair, mending.

So, when I saw Daddy heading out across the yard in the direction of the truck, I caught up with him and asked to tag along to town. I didn't ask Mama if I could go; she would have scolded me about neglecting the mending. I told Ruth instead to tell Mama that I had gone with Daddy. Ruth was playing with Miss Annie on the porch steps, surrounded by scattered doll clothes, off in her make-believe world as usual. There's no telling if she remembered to tell Mama.

When we got to Dalhart, we stopped at Joe Jennings's, the mechanic. Our old tractor had broken down again, and Daddy needed to order a new part. Mr. Jennings shook his head and told us it could be several weeks before the part arrives. With this Depression going on, everything seems to have slowed down. I hope for Daddy's sake that it comes in by the time planting season is here.

Daddy asked Mr. Jennings if he had an idea how much wheat seed would likely cost this spring. When he replied, I could see by the expression on Daddy's face that it was more than he could afford.

To make matters worse, Bud McCall, whose daughter Sadie is a constant burr under my saddle, joined the conversation. He agreed that seed prices are quite high, and *then* arrogantly asked Daddy if he needs a loan to plant this year. Daddy politely turned down Mr. McCall's offer. How does Daddy always answer people so nicely, even when he doesn't want to?

On the way home, I told Daddy one of his favorite jokes, the one about a farmer and his cow. He laughed, but not the same as he usually does. Daddy was quiet, which told me right away that he's worried.

Tuesday, February 26, 1935

This evening when Daddy talked to Mama about Bud McCall's offer for a seed loan, she bristled just as I had and declared that we don't need to borrow anything from the McCalls! As we sat down to supper, the matter was dropped until Mama softly, slowly asked Daddy if we have enough seed left over to plant this year's crop. He didn't respond for a moment, and then, without looking up from his plate, quietly answered, "I don't think so."

As I heard his words, an uneasy feeling settled in the pit

of my stomach. What will we do if we can't plant the spring wheat? Lord, I pray you'll make a way for Daddy, and please bring rain. Maybe then things will be back to normal — the way they used to be.

Wednesday, February 27, 1935

Mama had even *more* mending to be done this evening after supper. I was just beginning to repair a torn hem on one of Ruth's dresses, when we heard a knock on the back door. Mama called for the visitor to come on in and Helen came into the kitchen, her smile lighting up the room. We've been the best of friends ever since our very first day of school, when we made chains of yellow wildflowers under the elm tree.

Thankfully, Mama allowed me to take a break, and Helen and I raced off to the hayloft, our favorite spot. As we talked and laughed, the strain from Mama's chores and Ruth and everything else faded away. Helen confided to me she was more than happy to get away from *her* troubles — especially her two lazy older brothers. Helen loves to make me laugh by doing perfect imitations of Leroy and Chester.

My heart aches for the Walker family; Helen's daddy is held tightly in the grip of Bud McCall, renting one of his many tenant farms. Her mother and father tell her they must be polite and careful to not offend him, even though they don't have much regard for his way of doing things or how he treats people. Of course, Sadie McCall takes advantage of the situation, trying to rule over Helen. Somehow, Helen always keeps a smile.

Thursday, February 28, 1935

An *awful* day at school! It all started this morning during arithmetic. Sadie McCall had just correctly finished a problem on the blackboard and was smugly headed back to her seat when she bumped Helen's desk, spilling the inkwell! I could tell she did it on purpose. The black ink spilled over everything, making a big dark splotch on Helen's green calico dress, the one I know is her favorite. I could see tears beginning to spill down her cheeks while Sadie looked triumphant. Without thinking, I jumped to my feet and accused Sadie of purposely bumping Helen's desk. Sadie denied everything and said that Helen spilled the ink herself. One of Sadie's younger sisters chimed in and agreed that Sadie hadn't done a thing.

Miss Boston looked as if she didn't know what to do. She always seems reluctant to reprimand the McCalls. Helen and I've wondered if that's because Miss Boston's brother works for Bud McCall.

Miss Boston held up her hands, told everyone to settle down, and to just clean up the mess as quickly as possible. As the rest of the class returned to their arithmetic, Helen and I got on our hands and knees and scrubbed the ink off the floorboards. Helen gave me a grateful look; she was glad I had stood up for her, but when I glanced over at Sadie, she smirked haughtily. She's the worst!

Friday, March 1, 1935

Thankfully school today was peaceful and uneventful. Helen was much quieter than usual; I think she was still fretting about yesterday's incident with Sadie.

After school, I walked over the big hill and through the pasture to Helen's house, stopping on the way to pet our sweet red cow Rosie. I brought with me a little potted poppy that I've been growing indoors, one of the few things the dust hasn't yet destroyed. Poppies are Helen's favorite flowers — she says they look so happy. Hopefully it will help her feel that way, too.

Usually Helen comes to my house, and I can sort of see why. The Walkers' tenant farm is in a state of disarray, with pieces of wire and junk lying about the yard and a couple of scraggly chickens pecking the ground. Their only cow died right before Christmas, leaving them with no source of milk. I didn't see her father in sight; he must have been out in the field working. Mr. Walker usually doesn't have much to say, especially since times have gotten harder.

Suddenly, Leroy and Chester came running full-speed out the back door, probably to avoid doing chores. Helen tells me they do that quite a bit. When I walked into the kitchen, Helen was in the middle of washing a pile of dishes, up to her elbows in soap bubbles. Mrs. Walker was holding Helen's screaming baby sister, trying to quiet her while Henry, the five-year-old, was noisily playing with toy soldiers in the middle of the floor.

As I helped Helen dry the dishes, she told me her ruined dress is going to be cut up to make new dish towels. "At least it won't be wasted," she said sadly.

We then sat on the back steps and cuddled two of their new barn kittens. I dramatically suggested all sorts of ridiculous ideas to give Sadie back exactly what she deserved. The idea of placing a cow patty in Sadie's dinner pail made Helen giggle. I don't think I could actually go through with it, of course. Helen certainly couldn't; I think she remembers every Bible lesson we ever learned. By the time I left, our sides were sore from laughing at our wild notions. As I headed back home, I was even a bit more thankful for Mama's orderly ways at our house.

Saturday, March 2, 1935

The bitter, swirling winds have picked up with force once again to make up for the calm stillness of yesterday. I can taste the gritty dust between my teeth and feel it grinding under my feet as I walk across the floor — not the best conditions for making bread. Every dust particle seems to stick to the dough. We've all grown used to a little dirt in the bread, but on days like this the loaves turn out worse.

In a minute Mama will call me from my room to help her knead the dough as quickly as possible before too much dirt is mixed in. I'm still having difficulty kneading the dough inside a drawer, which does protect it from the gusts of dirt but is *terribly* bothersome if the drawer slides in and out or closes on my hands.

Sunday, March 3, 1935

Helen sang "It Is Well with My Soul" in church this morning, a beautiful hymn I've heard her sing many times. A contented hush fell over the sanctuary as her beautiful voice filled the room. By the time she finished, she was beaming, and several older ladies were wiping tears from their eyes. As I reached for my own handkerchief, I could feel the burdens I had carried with me through the church doors lifting from my soul, and my heart was freed. I don't know how I could ever endure these times without Helen.

After the service, Helen whispered that Sadie had made an ugly face at her when she returned to her seat after singing. It's no secret that Sadie can't carry a tune in a bucket.

I finished reading *Anne of Green Gables* this afternoon, snuggled in Daddy's favorite chair in front of the heat stove. Anne's story reminds me to be grateful for a family who loves and cares for me through both thick and thin. Like Mama, I plan to someday give it to my daughter to read, too. It's a wonderful book, my very favorite.

Tuesday, March 5, 1935

Mama told me today that I'd best hand down my smaller pair of overalls to Ruth before I wear out the seams. That leaves me only one pair now — if I grow any more, I won't have anything but my school dresses to wear for chores. Ruth complained and fussed about always getting my hand-me-downs until Mama reminded her that in Helen's family, overalls get passed down three or four times!

This morning on the way to school, Ruth and I noticed several of the neighboring wheat fields are nearly bare after yesterday's strong winds. Only a few lone, scraggly stalks of barely green wheat were left clinging to the ground. Dear Lord, help Daddy's remaining wheat continue to survive.

Wednesday, March 6, 1935

Daddy drove to town this afternoon to pick up a window-pane for Helen's daddy. The Walkers' kitchen window was shattered by a dead tree limb during the strong winds two days ago. To add to it all, Mr. Walker's old pickup won't start from being so clogged with dust.

I eagerly offered to milk Rosie and Dandelion while Daddy was gone helping the Walkers. It was much to Mama's reluctance, though — she was certain I'd get kicked, even though our sweet cows wouldn't hurt a fly. I've helped Daddy with the milking countless times, so Mama finally agreed.

The barn was warm and quiet and still. Pumpkin, the barn cat, waited patiently for her handout of warm milk, and Brownie snoozed on a pile of straw, wagging her tail from time to time. Gentle, red Rosie mooed and nudged me as I sat down to milk her.

It took me a good deal longer than it takes Daddy, and I probably spilled a bit more than he normally does, too. Mama didn't mind, though, and we poured the milk into large glass Mason jars after separating the cream. Ruth lugged the jars of milk and cream down the narrow stairs to the cool cellar, bellyaching all the while.

Daddy was surprised when I told him I'd done all the milking without any help. I could tell he was proud as he hugged me tightly, proclaiming, "That's my Grace!" Daddy always seems able to see my good intentions; how I wish Mama could see them, too!

Thursday, March 7, 1935

A duster hit today.

The afternoon had been beautifully warm, and Mama had even opened several windows in the house to let in the fresh air. Several ladies from church were over to discuss what could be done to help the community's less fortunate. After arriving home from school, I sat and listened to the conversation; Mama and the ladies seem to know every single family's needs.

Mrs. Mayfield's daughter Hannah came along with her to the meeting. She is Ruth's age, and they are two peas in a pod. The girls spent the whole afternoon out on the porch with their dolls. From time to time their laughter floated through the windows, and several ladies commented how nice it is to see carefree little girls like Hannah and Ruth.

Mama had just risen from her seat to make more coffee for the ladies when Ruth and Hannah burst in the front door, stammering about a big dark cloud coming fast. Looks of alarm traveled quickly around the room as the buzzing women grabbed their pocketbooks and rushed out to the porch.

Sure enough, an enormous cloud of yellowish-brown sand was sweeping toward the hill just beyond our farm. I gasped as the women ran to their automobiles and hurriedly drove away. Mama cried, "Dear Lord, help them make it home before it hits!" I shuddered, taking one last look at the cloud of sand — it was barreling ahead like a train, never slowing down.

Somehow, Ruth was once again absorbed with her doll, and I frantically grabbed her and stumbled into the house, shutting the door tightly. I had to urge her to help Mama and me soak sheets in water to hang over the windows and doors. We stuffed towels and rags along the windowsills to catch and filter out as much dirt as possible; without them, it's nearly impossible to breathe.

While Ruth placed sheets over our beds and pillows, I pushed a towel tightly under the last window, which was facing the wall of the coming storm. It sent chills down my back as I witnessed the mass of churning dust-fog hit the window right before my eyes with a deafening roar.

Ruth and I ran to the kitchen to join Mama, my hands trembling as the winds whipped against the walls, howling and whistling. There was no telling how long it would last, and as I sat down across the table from Mama, the room grew darker and darker, until finally I had to help Mama light the lamps.

Even though we had stuffed as many rags and towels against the panes as was possible, the windows still rattled noisily, and I feared any moment they would burst, letting in clouds of choking dust. As it was, there was dirt already seeping in through the cracks, and the room began to fill with foggy darkness. The glow of the lamp grew steadily dimmer, and Mama instructed Ruth and me to cover our noses. I was having trouble breathing even after I placed a damp handkerchief over my nose and mouth. One of these days, I fear our house will outright blow away with the rest of the swirling sand.

The door suddenly banged open in the wind, and I heard Daddy stumble in. I was so relieved he was safe; even though I knew he was just putting up the livestock, I'd worried he'd lost his way trying to make it to the house. He sat at the table with us to wait out the storm.

We sat in silence as the gusts of wind pounded our little house. It then became so dark, I couldn't see my hand as I stretched it out in front of my face. I kept drawing it nearer and nearer, but I couldn't see my fingers until they were only inches from my face. I knew that if I tried to talk no one would hear me over the deafening roar of the wind. I shut my stinging, burning eyes and buried my head in my arms — I could barely breathe, my eyes were on fire, and everything tasted and smelled like dust. I felt as if I were all alone.

I guess I fell asleep, because the next thing I knew, Mama was gently shaking me. I knew right away by the silence that the storm was over. Relief washed over me, like exhaustion after running a long, long race. Mama told me it was past 10:00 P.M. She gave me a piece of cornbread that she had wrapped up when the storm first hit, and told me we'll begin cleanup first thing in the morning. Tomorrow will be a day of hard work.

Friday, March 8, 1935

I ache all over so much; I don't even know exactly what it is that's aching. Mama called us early. I immediately got out of bed and was dressed soon after, but Ruth didn't even want to wake up. I dreaded having to spend a whole day away from school cleaning with Ruth and Mama.

First we strained the water. So much dirt and grit gets mixed in during a duster; it's impossible to get it all out. We had to pour it through a dishcloth several times to filter out the larger grains of sand. We then set it aside, allowing most of the remaining dirt to settle to the bottom. By suppertime, it was fit for use. It was still a little cloudy, but at least it tasted more like water than dust.

Dust covered the floor, and I spent nearly two hours sweeping every last corner, and whisking it out the door. Then Ruth and I proceeded to the front steps, which were completely covered in a huge sand dune. We scooped away, filling our buckets slowly. It didn't really matter where we dumped them, because most of the yard was covered with ripply waves of sand, anyway.

It seemed as if no matter how hard I worked, it was never satisfactory for Mama. I shoveled and swept the dirt off the porch, using lots of elbow grease. When Mama came to inspect, she said I needed to sweep the porch all over again, to rid it of the still-lingering grime. Sometimes I don't know which is worse: The dust storms or the cleaning.

Daddy spent a good deal of time unblocking the barn doors — the wind had blown a great mound of dirt right up to the door handles. He reported that his wheat had somehow stayed put in the ground, but he didn't know how. Meanwhile, Mama said the cupboards needed to be scrubbed, the sheets aired, and on and on her list continued.

By nightfall, we had just completed the last chore, and we were more than ready for bed. At least with Ruth already asleep beside me, I can write in my diary undisturbed.

Daddy said if the sandstorms keep coming this bad, we'll have to start going down in the cellar. I think these dusters wear down the people just as much as they wear down the land.

Saturday, March 9, 1935

Now that our own house is in Mama's apple-pie order, she immediately suggested this morning we check in on the Mayfields to see how they're faring. I wanted to stop by and see how Helen was after the storm, but Mama said visiting the Mayfields was more urgent.

They didn't have much time at all to prepare for this last dust storm; I imagine they barely made it home before it hit. Mama prepared a basked filled with hot biscuits to take to their family.

All the way to the Mayfields', the road was covered in big drifts of sand. It was like driving over a thousand little hills, and my hind end is thoroughly sore from hitting the seat time after time. Ruth was absolutely infuriating — she laughed every time we hit a bump, and even on a smooth stretch, she purposefully bounced in her seat and giggled.

I'd had all I could take by the time we reached the Mayfields' farm — especially when Mama asked why I was frowning and acting as though I had a "bee in my bonnet"!

Things weren't as bad as we had feared, but the Mayfields' conditions were decidedly worse than at our farm. Ruth took along her doll, Miss Annie, and played with Hannah while we helped the Mayfields with the remaining cleanup needing to be done. Mrs. Mayfield then insisted we stay a little longer to enjoy Mama's biscuits with her delicious peach preserves.

Sunday, March 10, 1935

In church this morning, we could barely hear Pastor Benson's sermon over the ruckus of the howling wind.

Sadie *and* her two sisters *and* her mama had on brand-new dresses and looked terribly showy. I can't imagine! Four new dresses in one family, and it's not even Easter or Christmas. Ruth and I haven't had a new dress the past *two* Christmases and Easters. Daddy tells us that with the next big wheat harvest, we'll go to church wearing new dresses, too. I told Helen I sometimes almost wish my daddy were a rich rancher, like Sadie's, who rents out land to tenant farmers. Then I could buy new dresses "just because" and live in a big, strong house that keeps out a good deal of the dust.

Helen said it wouldn't be worth it to have to act like the McCalls. I suppose she's right.

After arriving home from morning services, we found everything in the house covered in layers of fine sandy dust. Apparently the back door blew open in the ferocious wind.

It seemed odd to be doing chores on Sunday. But nonetheless, Mama and I spent almost the whole afternoon sweeping and recleaning the house. The work was exhausting, and every limb on my body is aching sore again. Ruth poked along, as usual, which did nothing to help the situation. She hauled the buckets outside to dump them — for a little while. Then she began making piles of dirt and sticking twigs on top like little sand castles.

I'm fed up with this dust. Even Sundays aren't days of rest anymore.

Monday, March 11, 1935

Sadie was once again boasting loudly at school how her house is electrically powered. The McCalls' large house is near enough to the main highway to connect to the power lines. Sadie *delights* in the fact that no one else at school has electricity. She and her sisters take great pride in being the only ones not living in town who can listen to radio dramas and have instant lighting. Goodness, when Mama was growing up in Fort Worth, she had electrical power *and* indoor plumbing, *and* a telephone, and I've yet to hear her boast about it to anyone!

Bread making today was a little easier since the wind was quieter than it's been in weeks. Mama even said to knead the dough on the countertop rather than in the drawer. The aroma of fresh bread filled the house, and Daddy perked right up when he stepped inside at suppertime and smelled the loaves. I could hear him softly whistling as he washed up for supper.

We used the last of the flour, so Mama will wash and dry the cotton flour sack to make my new underclothes. At first, the fabric is itchy, but after a week or so, it's more wearable.

Tuesday, March 12, 1935

A barn owl has moved into our barn! Daddy saw him fly into the rafters this morning as the owl returned from his nightly hunting. He's living up in the highest part of the rafters in the back of the barn. Mama said a barn owl is wonderful to have around to keep down the mice.

We all went very quietly into the barn to look at him. He turned his head completely around, or so it seemed, to look down at us with his big, round eyes. Ruth and I want to think up a name for him. I hope he stays awhile.

Wednesday, March 13, 1935

We went to a special midweek prayer service tonight. Pastor Benson felt like our area needed to have a time of prayer for the farmers and their families. Even with so many chores to be done, Daddy suggested it would be "just the lift our souls need," so we went.

Pastor Benson's message was about hope, and continuing on when faced with impossible situations. I think everyone listened to each and every word he said. As the congregation stood after the closing prayer, I saw that Daddy stayed on his knees a little bit longer, his eyes closed and his hands clasped, deep in prayer.

Thursday, March 14, 1935

After supper I hid in the hayloft to watch the barn owl fly out to begin his hunting. I didn't tell Ruth where I was going, or she would have begged to come along. Ruth insists on calling the owl "Speckles," because she says his face is covered in freckles.

He flew right over my hiding spot in the corner, and his powerful wings sent a slight breeze across the hayloft, gently blowing the loose straw on the floor. He gave a little hoot and joined the crescent moon as he flew away.

Friday, March 15, 1935

Helen's coming over after school today! Both of our mamas agreed she could walk home with me after school and stay the night, provided Helen had all her chores finished.

Bedtime

Oh, what a time we've had! After school, Helen and I climbed up in the hayloft, seated on thrones of golden, sweet-smelling straw — all we have left from the last year's meager wheat crop. Helen said she felt like the princess in "Rumpelstiltskin," surrounded with straw to weave into gold.

Pumpkin has her newest baby kittens hidden in the corner. There's a fluffy orange tabby, a white one with gray patches, and the little runt is black flecked with tiny orange dots. Brownie, oddly enough, is crazy over the kittens. She licks them as if she were their mother. Pumpkin doesn't tolerate it for too long, though.

Helen told me about the newspaper ad announcing a new upcoming serial story. It sounds exciting, but Mama and Daddy tell Ruth and me that the stories they put in the paper nowadays are pure rubbish, and proper young ladies don't read such things. Helen confided that she wishes she could read just one, and I had to admit I agreed. Sadie McCall reads each and every one of them, and comes to school loudly discussing the latest episode just because she *knows* Helen and I aren't allowed to read them.

We heard Daddy come through the creaky wooden barn doors below us to milk Rosie and Dandelion. He was whistling "Texas, Our Texas," his very favorite tune. Daddy hollered up to the hayloft, "If you princesses are still up there, it's nearly time for supper!"

We're in bed peacefully now, due to the fact Ruth is sleeping with Daddy and Mama tonight. I seldom try to write in bed; it's nearly impossible with Ruth peeking over my shoulder or trying to observe where I tuck away my diary. Helen would never do anything like that.

Mama and Daddy are talking in the kitchen and will probably come shortly to tell us to blow out the lamp. I heard Daddy walking toward our room now. Good night!

Saturday, March 16, 1935

Helen and I had a good dose of morning entertainment before breakfast! She and I were giggling as we carried the buckets of fresh milk from the barn. Daddy had kept us amused while he milked, squirting milk into Pumpkin's waiting mouth.

From seemingly out of nowhere, Ruth appeared behind us, shouting, "The British are coming! The British are coming!" at the top of her lungs. I suppose Ruth overheard the older students' Revolutionary War lesson at school.

I jumped, whirled around, and lost my grip on the bucket, sending it flying in Ruth's direction. She yelped and, covered in fresh milk, fled toward the house. On the way, she tripped and fell flat on her face in a mound of dirt, becoming a human mud pie.

Mama came rushing outside to see what was causing all the commotion, while Ruth just lay helplessly on the ground. It was hilarious, and Helen and I burst out laughing. We had tears in our eyes by the time Mama helped her up, and Ruth remarked in a pout, "Well, I guess Paul Revere probably *was* a little dirty after riding so long, don't you think?"

The whole incident would have been even funnier if I hadn't been given Ruth's chores to do for the rest of the day. Mama wasn't pleased that I didn't help Ruth after she fell.

Since the wind and dust were quickly stirring up, Mrs. Walker sent over Leroy and Chester shortly after breakfast to drive Helen home. Helen rolled her eyes as they impatiently honked the horn.

Mama carefully fixed a box with a dozen eggs and two Mason jars of milk for Helen's family. The two boys hollered out the truck's open windows for Helen to hurry it up. I'm happy as a lark to not have any brothers. I could never handle two brothers *and* Ruth!

Sunday March 17, 1935

The wind is ferocious! It was so bad that before Ruth and I awoke, Mama came into our bedroom from the kitchen and told us we wouldn't be able to go to Sunday school or church services this morning. We both quickly dressed in our overalls rather than Sunday clothes and went in to help Mama with breakfast. She already had it fixed and hurriedly informed us that we were going to wait out the storm in the tiny cellar, where the dust would be less fierce.

Mama handed us damp handkerchiefs to cover our mouths and noses as we filed down into the underground room. I could see Mama was worried — I think she was just as afraid as Ruth and I were.

Without windows and with only one door, the small cellar wasn't nearly as dusty as the house, but it was still difficult to breathe. After a short while, Daddy joined us. We ate our breakfast of biscuits in silence. Mama then attempted to read us our Sunday school lesson over the ruckus of the wind.

Daddy and Mama sat in the two rickety chairs around the small table where Mama had set the lamp. Daddy read yesterday's paper while Mama tried to write a letter to Granny and Granddaddy in Fort Worth. All the while, the wind was howling without end, and dust continued to float about in the air. Finally, after what seemed like an eternity of silence, Ruth asked Daddy to read a Bible story. So for the rest of the morning, Daddy, in a strong, loud voice, read all our favorites from the big, worn Bible.

Suppertime

It's nearly five o'clock now, and the wind hasn't let up all day. Lord, please watch over the livestock; keep Brownie and Pumpkin safe in the barn, and Speckles, too — poor owl! How I hope this wind has almost blown itself out — surely after this many hours there can't be much breath left in the storm! The last of our dried beef is down here in the cellar; that and leftover biscuits will more than likely be our supper.

There goes Ruth; she's asking Mama if we can act out the Bible stories Daddy read to us; she's looking my way, and I imagine I'm fixing to be cast as a character in her play. I'll write later.

Monday, March 18, 1935

We slept on the cellar floor last night, using the spare quilts Mama stores down there. When we finally crawled out this morning, it was as if we had stepped into a whole different world. Huge mounds of sand had piled up against the side of the house, reaching as high as the roof. The barn was in the same condition — the entire north side couldn't be seen at all. The top of Daddy's tractor was just visible above a monstrous sand drift. Daddy sighed and remarked that he should have parked it on the other side of the barn.

Daddy headed straight to the barn to check the livestock, and right away Mama organized the cleanup in the house. It didn't really matter where we dumped the reddish dirt. The whole Panhandle looked as if it needed a good sweeping!

Ruth and I went out to unclog the water flow from the windmill and worked on filling up the largest tub with water. I heard the beating of a horse's hooves on the sand and looked up to see Hannah Mayfield's father galloping toward the barn as quickly as his horse could manage. The loose dust billowed around him like fog, making it look as if he were floating on a cloud. Daddy and Mama rushed over to him.

After a brief conversation, Daddy hurried into the pickup and drove off, with Mr. Mayfield and his horse not far behind. Mama came walking back toward us. Her face grim, she explained that the Mayfields' roof caved in over the kitchen this morning from the weight of all the dirt. Imagine your roof just falling down!!! To make matters worse, the Mayfields' truck wouldn't start from being choked with dirt. Daddy's there now helping, and Mama, Ruth, and I will be going later to help Mrs. Mayfield clean her house. He says we all have to keep helping each other persevere.

Tuesday, March 19, 1935

We had to miss yet another day of school to help with the cleanup. Mama said she didn't imagine Miss Boston would even try to conduct classes.

It took Daddy, Mr. Mayfield, and a couple of other men all day yesterday to repair the Mayfields' roof. Mama, Ruth, Hannah, Mrs. Mayfield, and I tried to clean as much as possible, but with the doors opening and closing continually and the dirt that kept falling through the tattered roof, we declared it a lost cause and quit until the men had finished. Hannah coughed every time a breeze brought more dust through the open doors and windows.

Mrs. Mayfield seemed a little downcast. Everything was covered in thick dust. The house, the furniture and even Mrs. Mayfield's blue dress looked worn out and faded. When we were fixing to leave, Mrs. Mayfield held up her head and told us all, "I'm looking forward to the day when the rain decides to come. It sure will help out things around here, won't it?" I thought to myself, *the rain* will *come; it* has *to come.*

Wednesday, March 20, 1935

Since Ruth and I had worked diligently at our house and the Mayfields' for two days, Mama felt it best that we return to school today.

Hardly a soul was there, almost as if everyone had been blown away with the wind. Miss Boston assured us that most everyone's still busy trying to get things back in order after such a devastating duster. I suppose that's where Helen was.

At recess, Betsy Payton told me she'd heard nearly the entire Stratford family has taken ill with pneumonia — not just pneumonia, but *dust* pneumonia. I'd never heard of such a thing, but Betsy explained that breathing in so much dust can make people too sick to do anything. The Stratford children have been coughing up clods of dirt. How terrible!

Thursday, March 21, 1935

Ruth and I started out walking to school, with the wind whipping our dresses and hair and the dust so thick, we could hardly see from one fence post to the next. Daddy wouldn't have it, though, and drove us to school — something he's never done before!

When we arrived, I could see Helen first thing, her hair glowing a brilliant red through the hazy dust as she entered the schoolhouse. I was relieved to see her. I know it seems silly, but after what Betsy told me about the Stratford family, I was scared to death Helen had come down with dust pneumonia. I gave a silent prayer of thanks for Helen and her friendship.

Everyone seemed to have the same dismal report — hardly any wheat remains in the fields, near and far. Daddy quietly told us at supper that his two fields protected by the hill are all he has left now. He'll be grateful to get three or four bushels an acre. To think only a few years ago Daddy harvested close to sixty bushels of wheat an acre from the same land.

Friday, March 22, 1935

Hannah Mayfield met us on the way to school this morning. She and Ruth chattered away and played in the huge sand dunes that had collected along the fencerows and ditches from Sunday's sandstorm. Just as I was wondering to myself why little Hannah had gone out of her way to walk with us, Ruth asked that very question.

Hannah explained that her mama said she'd nearly had "heart failure" after this last big duster. By the expression on her face, I could tell Hannah didn't quite seem to know what that was. In the event another duster hits while she's walking to or from school, her mama doesn't want Hannah to be alone. So Hannah promised her mama she'd walk with us from now on.

When we reached the schoolyard, Helen met me with an unhappy expression. Her mama said she's *got* to walk with both Leroy and Chester in case another big duster hits. The last thing Helen wants to do is tag along behind her older brothers every day! I don't blame her in the least: Leroy, the oldest, is as boastful as the day is long. Chester follows right in his steps. They rarely help out as they should on the farm. My daddy would *never* put up with boys like Leroy and Chester!

Betsy Payton joined in our conversation. Betsy always

speaks her mind, which usually winds up leaving everyone in stitches. More than once she's gotten into a pinch for being so opinionated, and Helen or I've had to come to her rescue.

Suddenly, the sound of horses' hooves caused everyone to look up. What do you know, Sadie and her two sisters pranced up on three of her father's beautiful white mares, their noses held high. Several of the boys rushed over — the McCall ranch has some of the finest horses in the Texas Panhandle. Helen rolled her eyes, and Betsy spouted out, "What possible good is a horse if a duster hits?" Helen shook her head as she commented that she reckoned it'd get Sadie and her sisters home faster.

Saturday, March 23, 1935

This evening after supper, I took the slop bucket and soured milk out to feed the hogs. As I came in the back door, I could hear Mama's and Daddy's voices in the front room, low so as not to be easily heard. Mama sounded extremely worried, and Daddy was quiet, so I imagine he was fretting, too. I know better than to eavesdrop, but as I swept the kitchen, I carefully listened.

Daddy told Mama how the banks are giving loans right and left for farmers to buy seed and then pay back at harvest time — if they get a crop. It seems everyone has Daddy's same problem of being short on wheat seed and money. There have just been too many bad years in a row. Mama said something about mortgages and other financial things I didn't quite understand. Daddy mentioned about his tractor part still not coming in.

I pray every night for Daddy. I know how hard these times are on him. Mama's told us many times how before she and Daddy were married, he worked two jobs in the city to save up money. She says it was the happiest day of his life when he bought a team of horses and this farm. It's always been his dream to have his own land. "It's just in his blood," she says.

Sunday, March 24, 1935

Dark gray clouds moved in just as the morning worship service began. We were all hoping they held rain, even Pastor Benson, who prayed especially long at the close of the service for this drought to come to an end.

Bedtime

It rained!! As soon as the sprinkles began this afternoon, Daddy picked up Mama and whirled her around — we could barely contain ourselves. The rain gauge measured a mere quarter inch, but maybe, just maybe, it will rain again — soon — and this drought will be a memory.

Monday, March 25, 1935

Young Adam Stratford came to school crying. Some of the boys made fun of him until he angrily told them why — his mother died Sunday morning of dust pneumonia. That stunned them into silence, and they left him alone the rest of the day.

Mama and several of the ladies from church are doing whatever they can to help the poor Stratford family. There's no school tomorrow morning, because the schoolhouse will be needed for the funeral services. Mama said the newspaper has accounts of someone dying from dust pneumonia almost every week.

Tuesday, March 26, 1935

On the way home from school, Ruth and I heard shots being fired. There wasn't anyone in sight, but we both figured someone was shooting at a jackrabbit for supper.

We were still a good mile from home when an old pickup went rattling past, covering us in dust. I was mortified when

I saw at least ten scrawny cattle carcasses piled in the back, shot dead. Ruth started crying when she saw the dead cows, and we hurried home to ask Mama and Daddy about it.

At supper, Daddy explained that many farmers can't afford to feed their cattle, and the animals are in too poor a condition to be sold at market. So President Roosevelt started a new program to pay farmers $3 to buy a calf and $16 for a cow. The awful thing about the government program, though, is the cattle are shot and then hauled off or burned. Mama said it's a crying shame to think of all that beef going to waste with so many people starving.

Ruth asked if Rosie or Dandelion was going to be shot, too, but Daddy assured both of us that we'd do no such thing. Daddy's still able to feed them well, keeping them nice and fat. He said it was a smart thing that he sold off his dozen or so beef steers last fall while they were still fat and healthy. They brought enough money to keep Rosie and Dandelion well fed throughout this winter.

Daddy said that although the government program just started, people are already complaining about the wasted meat. It doesn't make any sense for cattle to be slaughtered and then just thrown away.

I don't like how things are changing. Part of me wants to break loose and cry: the starving cattle, the discouraged farmers, the little children without supper tonight. Another part of me is beginning to live in fear of this Depression. Each day seems to bring a little more hardship for someone.

Wednesday, March 27, 1935

From the minute I arrived at school, every conversation concerned this week's captivating chapter of the newspaper serial. The heroine of the story was in a terrible dilemma, and the end of the chapter left the reader hanging.

I gathered this much just by listening to Sadie gush about how "Constance Chatelaine just *can't* die; that would be *too, too* awful!!" By the end of the day, Helen and I were sick of all the serial talk — it's not even a real person or story. I hope by next week, "Constance Chatelaine" is saved and lives happily ever after — just to spare Helen and me from having to listen to every girl in the school carrying on!

Thursday, March 28, 1935

Helen discovered an old hat of her mama's stuffed in the bottom of a trunk yesterday afternoon while she was looking for a clean handkerchief. It was trimmed with beautiful yellow ribbon, along with several ugly yellow flowers. She pulled off the ribbon and wore it in her hair today. It complements her auburn hair beautifully, and matches her one remaining school dress.

This evening I peeked in a few of Mama's trunks, but I didn't find any old hats with ribbons to spare. Helen's lucky — a brand-new hair ribbon, and it didn't cost her a cent!

Friday, March 29, 1935

Just before she dismissed class for the day, Miss Boston said she had a happy announcement that would help lift our spirits: the upcoming annual End of School Festival! After school is dismissed for the summer, an entire afternoon is filled with games, music, a picnic, and, as the grand finale, the schoolwide Dramatic Competition.

As soon as the words had left Miss Boston's mouth, the room began to buzz, and it took several minutes to restore order. Helen, Betsy, Abigail, Mary, and I agreed to once again perform together for this year's competition. We've entered together the past two years — and *won*. Helen and I had the leading roles, and the audience laughed and sighed in exactly the right places. It was one of the best moments ever to win for the second year running — especially since

Sadie's group received *second* place both times. Last year, I couldn't help feeling smug the next day at church when I noticed Sadie seemed sulky. That made victory all the sweeter.

Saturday, March 30, 1935

Mama said it's a good thing that tonight is our weekly bath, because I am completely covered from head to foot in sand and dust! Ruth warted me endlessly to play "Sahara Desert" in the mountainous sand dunes. I was reluctant at first, but it turned out to be great fun. We raced each other down the big hill, which was covered in blown sand. Once, on the way to the bottom, Ruth fell and slid all the way down.

For the remainder of the afternoon we "sledded" down the slope using a loose board from the barn. When we'd explained to Daddy why we needed it, he couldn't hold back the smile that spread across his face. Daddy hugged Ruth and me tightly, saying we know how to make the best out of what the good Lord's given us.

Sunday, March 31, 1935

I saw the most *amazing* thing when Mama asked me to haul in water from the windmill! As I filled the bucket with cool water from the tank, I happened to glance up to the tip-top of the windmill's frame, not far from the slowly spinning blades. To my surprise, a crow had built its nest there — *using bits of baling wire and barbed wire!* I ran to the barn where Daddy was fixing to start milking. He followed me to the windmill and looked in disbelief when he saw the huge wire nest. He told me to run get Mama to come look.

Mama, with Ruth tagging along, came hurrying out to where Daddy stood. Ruth squealed as we looked at the crow's nest, both puzzled by the oddity of it, and entertained by the humorous spectacle. Daddy merrily whistled as he climbed up the windmill and gently pulled it loose from the wooden frame. Making his way slowly downward, I looked over at Ruth, whose eyes were huge.

We all crowded around to look at the nest — it was made mostly of wire and tumbleweed twigs. The inside was delicately lined with fluffy little black feathers and pieces of dried prairie grass. Needless to say, the crow's nest was *very* secure! There were still tiny bits of the hatched eggs left inside. I guess even the crows are having a hard time when there's not enough grass or twigs for nest building.

Monday, April 1, 1935

Helen couldn't believe it when I told her about the crow's nest — she thought I was April-fooling her. Her mama might let her come over this week to look at it, if the wind and dust aren't blowing too badly. Ruth wanted to bring the nest to school, but Daddy said no. I think he just figured that for Ruth, it isn't safe to be toting around a big ball of wire.

Tuesday, April 2, 1935

Red Cross volunteers came to school to hand out dust masks. A stern older lady explained in detail the importance of wearing them. She briskly demonstrated how to properly wear the masks over our mouths and noses.

Ruth and a couple of the other little girls perched the white cotton masks on top of their heads as "nurse caps." Before I could give Ruth a serious glare, Miss Boston cleared her throat and raised her eyebrows until order was restored.

Miss Boston instructed everyone to hang their mask on a hook in the cloakroom, where they are within easy reach if another dust storm barrels across the plains while we are in school.

I think having the Red Cross visit the school made us

older students realize how dangerous these dusters are to our health. Although the dust masks were given out to provide protection, they seemed to make everyone a little uneasier.

Wednesday, April 3, 1935

Mama's fit to be tied because Ruth left the chicken coop unlatched last night. Coyotes got at least five of the hens, and now we won't have nearly as many eggs to sell in town. This afternoon, Daddy fastened one end of a heavy rope to the back door and the other end to the barn door handles, like a giant jump rope. He said that during dust storms, the rope will help guide him to and from the barn.

Thursday, April 4, 1935

Helen, Betsy, Abigail, Mary, and I spent all afternoon after school up in Betsy's big, secluded attic writing our script for the Dramatic Competition. The gusty wind outside rattled the dusty windowpanes and covered any noise we could have possibly made! Each group likes to keep their script a secret until the day of the performance. I'm not even going to chance writing what ours is about, just in case Ruth peeks in my diary. I will say, however, that this is the best drama we've ever written!

Friday, April 5, 1935

Daddy, Mama, Ruth, and I all piled into the truck after school and drove to town. Daddy's been fretting more each day about the part he needs to fix the tractor still not arriving, especially since just about every other farmer has begun plowing their fields to prepare for spring wheat planting. He dropped us off at the Piggly Wiggly and headed to the mechanic's.

While we were busy buying flour, coffee, and other necessities, I overheard the grocer talking in low tones to another customer at the cash register. They were bitterly complaining how the farmers are to blame for these dusters growing worse, what with the way they stay out on their tractors day and night plowing the fields and adding more clouds of dust to the already dirt-choked skies.

I heard the grocer darkly remark, "These days, with most of the farmers owning tractors, there's just too much plowing going on. The rate they're going, all the life will be blown out of Dalhart within the next ten years, and we'll be part of the New Mexico desert before we know what happened."

Daddy's solemn expression when he picked us up at the Piggly Wiggly told me the tractor part still hasn't arrived. I pondered the storekeeper's remark as we drove back home.

I know the plowing night and day *does* stir up more dust to feed the dusters, but will it really cause the Panhandle to turn into a desert?

Saturday, April 6, 1935

At last Helen was able to visit and see the wire crow's nest. She marveled at it just as we had and said her daddy recently heard about the same kind of nest being found high in a tree near Amarillo.

We spent the rest of the afternoon up in the hayloft talking, safely hidden from Ruth. Helen said she'd heard Sadie boasting to Miss Boston about the fashion magazines her mother receives in the mail every month. Fashion magazines! I can never see Mama wasting good money on such a thing. Helen's daddy won't even spend money on a newspaper.

Helen shook her head and said what's even more ridiculous is that Sadie and her sisters cut out any pictures of handsome men in the magazines and paste them in a scrapbook! And their mama allows it! Helen and I both agreed that a picture can't truly say much about how a boy *really* is. I smiled and told Helen my daddy might not be handsome enough to be in Sadie's scrapbook, but the man *I* marry will have to be a lot like him in every other way.

Helen stayed on for supper, and afterward Mama sent

her home with three jars of milk and two pounds of butter. Helen hugged Mama with a grateful smile.

Thankfully, Ruth has finally dozed off to sleep now and won't keep pestering me about what I'm writing. Just as I was about to snap at her about how lucky Sadie and her sisters are to each have their *own* bedrooms, I thought of how Helen never even complains about her whole family sleeping in one room. Seven people sharing one room! The Walkers' small tenant house has two rooms, and Helen's mama and daddy are the only ones who even have a real bed. The children make do with worn-out mattresses on the cold floor.

Now I can understand why Mama is always proud to remind us how hard Daddy worked the summer after Ruth was born building a new little bedroom onto our house for "his girls." Help me, dear Lord, to be more grateful.

Sunday, April 7, 1935

The Ladies Auxiliary hosted a covered-dish noon dinner after morning services. The weather and the wind cooperated so it could be held outdoors as planned.

We brought an extra-big pot of Mama's heavenly chicken and dumplings. Mama kept threatening that our meanest rooster, Prince Charming, was going to wind up in a pot of dumplings, and she finally kept her word.

The serving tables overflowed with everyone's favorites, but it was Mama's chicken and dumplings that brought all the men back for seconds and even thirds until it was all gone. Sadie McCall waited until I glanced in her direction, then made a horrid face and dramatically spit out a mouthful. I *know* she was just plain acting and trying to get my temper up, because I've never heard of a soul disliking Mama's chicken and dumplings as long as I've lived!

I noticed Helen's family didn't bring any food, and I overheard Mama trying to convince Mrs. Walker that was no cause for their family not to stay and eat. I may just be borrowing trouble, but I worry Helen's been looking thin lately, and at school she hasn't brought much to eat in her dinner pail.

Monday, April 8, 1935

We held play practice this afternoon in our hayloft — it was a bit disorganized, but it always is the first few times. Mama even brought up a plate of warm molasses cookies. If I could, I'd spend all day practicing the play up in the hayloft.

The afternoon would have been perfect if it hadn't been for one thing: Helen couldn't come. Her mama had told her to get home right after school to help with the younger children and the chores. Helen seemed on the verge of tears when she told me.

Tuesday, April 9, 1935

Speckles left us. He didn't return from his nightly hunting two days ago, and we are fairly certain he's gone for good. The barn cats will have to work overtime to keep up with the mice and rats now!

Ruth cried when she realized that Speckles had disappeared. She insisted that we search to find him, until Mama gently explained that Speckles was just doing what came naturally.

Wednesday, April 10, 1935

During noontime at school, we were forced to stay inside. The wind started late last night and hasn't let up since. I shuddered every time I took a bite of my cornbread, hearing and feeling the inevitable crunch of sand between my teeth.

Since outdoor activities were out of the question, Miss Boston suggested we gather into our groups and discuss our drama presentations for the End of School Festival. Our group gathered in a corner and talked over costumes, props, and scenery. We decided to each come up with a costume idea tonight and tell what we found tomorrow at noon.

Daddy had to pick up Ruth and me after school again in the truck. When we arrived home, Mama was busy in the kitchen attempting to strain a jar of water. I excitedly told her about needing a costume, but when I asked for ideas, she quickly shook her head and told me I'd be on my own putting one together this year.

I remember the past two years, when Mama joined me in my quest for a costume as soon as supper was finished and the dishes put away. We'd rummage through closets and chests, dreaming up all sorts of possibilities, giggling over our ideas.

For almost an hour tonight, I searched the house but didn't come up with a costume. It's just not the same.

Thursday, April 11, 1935

As Ruth, Hannah, and I walked past one of the Mayfields' remaining winter wheat fields on the way to school, we saw a jackrabbit hungrily nibbling the scraggly wheat. I shooed it away, and Ruth scowled that I would deprive a starving little jackrabbit. I told her that once the farmers' families have food on their tables, *then* we could worry about feeding all the Panhandle's jackrabbits.

Every day now, Daddy faithfully pushes his finger down into the earth, checking to see if the soil is warm enough yet to plant the spring wheat. More than half of our three hundred acres sits bare and empty, waiting for the spring wheat to be planted, while the remaining acres of sparse winter wheat are barely thriving without any moisture. I don't think the stalks are even six inches high, and I wonder how much will even be left to harvest come June.

I've never seen Daddy so worried and quiet. The spring wheat can't be planted until the fields are all plowed. And the fields can't be plowed until the tractor is fixed. Sometimes I see him standing out in the fields, deep in thought, Brownie at his side.

I'm going to keep praying long and hard for Daddy and Mama — and Helen, too. Helen's been so quiet at school lately and not her usual smiling self. Today she brought half of a biscuit in her dinner pail and wouldn't take any of the cornbread or sausage I offered.

Carefree Ruth seems to be the only person I know who isn't acting differently. But then, it would take nothing short of a catastrophe to cause Ruth to fret!

Friday, April 12, 1935

Sadie's younger sister, Sophie, brought the newspaper to school with the final chapter of the serial that's been running for weeks now. A lot of the girls read it during noontime and cried at the end; I suppose someone died.

Ruth was a little grumbly that she hadn't been allowed to

read it and keep up with what all the older girls were talking about. I think she plans on trying to convince Mama and Daddy to let her read the next serial that comes along, but I doubt she'll have any luck.

Truth be told, I was actually glad to hear about something other than the blowing wind and sandstorms.

Saturday, April 13, 1935

I feel as if my life has changed into its own swirling, confused sandstorm, arriving suddenly and sweeping away all happiness in its disorder. I've encountered the worst imaginable blow.

This morning I headed to Helen's house, hoping to have a good, long visit about what's got her so down-hearted lately. I wasn't prepared, though, for what I found.

As I approached the front door, I saw it hanging wide open, revealing the bare and empty room beyond as it banged lightly against the house in the wind. I hurried around to the back just in time to see Helen sadly crawling into the back of their old truck, which was piled high: a mattress, a table, an old washtub, a broom, and just about anything else their family owns.

I frantically called out to Helen. She turned and saw me, and for a moment her face brightened. Helen began to crawl back out of the truck, then hesitantly looked over at her father. He nodded, and my friend flew toward me, the dust billowing in clouds beneath her feet.

"Oh, Grace!" she exclaimed. "I was wishing I could see you just one last time before we left." Helen couldn't hide the tears filling her eyes and spilling onto her cheeks. "Daddy said we just can't hang on anymore," she sobbed, twisting her worn handkerchief in her hands. "So now we're moving away to California. Imagine, Grace! All the way to California!" She explained how a man had told her daddy that California's the only place with jobs, untouched by the Depression.

Helen's father gently called her back to the truck, reminding her that they wanted to travel as far as possible before nightfall.

Helen hugged me tightly. Tears clogged my throat, and I couldn't speak a word. With all the hope she could muster, Helen promised solemnly, "I'll come back someday, Grace — maybe after the dust decides to stop blowing. And I'll write as soon as I can rustle up a pen and paper!"

"Good-bye, Helen!" I cried as she crawled back into the truck and began to drive away. She stuck her head around the mattress, and we waved until the old pickup puffed and sputtered over the horizon hazy with dust.

I stood in disbelief for the longest time and then finally

walked slowly back home, my tears leaving a trail behind me — drops of sorrow in the parched dust.

My mind feels blank — I don't know what I'll do without Helen, my dearest companion for more than half my life. Yet, at the same time, I'm truly startled. I know the storms are bad, and the Depression is causing lots of folks to go without, but I'd thought surely things would begin improving. I just can't believe Helen's family has let go of their last thread of hope here in Dalhart.

Sunday, April 14, 1935

I awoke this morning before the sun came up, still exhausted from crying so much last night. I can't bear the thought of leaving for morning services shortly and not seeing Helen there like always. My eyes so easily fill with tears; even after I was sure that last night I'd cried every tear I had in me. I'm smudging the ink; I'll quit writing now. There's really nothing more to say, anyway.

Evening

Death is surely coming for us — how will we survive? I will try writing to help occupy this terrorizing time of waiting.

Despite my gloominess, the weather for this Palm

Sunday began incredibly beautiful. The sky was crystal blue — not a puff of dust in the air. It felt better than anything in the world to breathe clean, fresh air and feel stillness rather than raging wind. It helped to refresh my mind. Pastor Benson's assuring words during the sermon served to soothe my spirit a little.

This evening after the Sunday supper dishes were washed and dried, Mama asked Ruth to take the wet dish towels outside to the clothesline to dry while I swept and Mama put away the pots and pans.

Suddenly out of nowhere, a storm grew on the horizon — a duster bigger and blacker than any we had ever seen. Mama sent Ruth to quickly pull the dish towels off the clothesline while Daddy rushed to the barn to secure the livestock and Brownie. I quickly helped Mama hang dampened sheets in the doorways and windows, a routine all too familiar.

After a few minutes, Ruth had still not returned and Mama sent me to tell her to hurry. When I stepped outside, only one towel was flapping in the growing wind. I scouted the yard and barn, hollering loudly for her.

I panicked and I ran over the hill, searching. To my relief, Ruth was a few hundred yards away chasing after a blowing white towel. I cried out her name and ran all the way to her. When I reached my sister, she looked up at me with fear in her bright blue eyes. I tried to hide the fact that I, too, was scared of the approaching storm, boiling black as night in the sky. Ruth started to explain about the runaway towel, but I told her there wasn't time. By now we were far from the house, and the storm was rolling closer and closer, swallowing up the sky as it came. I knew we couldn't make it home.

Desperately, I looked and saw, not far away, Helen's abandoned house, with the door still open and banging in the wind. I grabbed Ruth's hand, pulled her to her feet, and together we ran with all our might to Helen's house. We raced inside, slamming and locking the door behind us. I scanned the room for a place to hide, but it was bare. I scooped up Ruth, who was crying on the floor, and rushed into a corner. I pulled her down to the dusty wooden floorboards and put the damp towel she was still clutching over our noses and mouths, preparing for the worst. It was then that I realized my diary was still snug in my dress pocket from earlier this morning.

The storm is now so close, I can feel it. The air has grown chilly, and the wind has, strangely, died. The world is deadly silent as Ruth and I huddle here together, praying prayer after prayer. The suspense is terrible as we wait.

Thousands of birds have filled the sky, fleeing ahead of the storm, calling as they fly. This is a nightmare too terrifying to be true! I'm crying along with Ruth and wishing we were at home in the cellar with Mama and Daddy.

I can see out a small window across the room as a towering mountain of black reaches into the dark sky. An eerie, pale yellow fog hovers above, crowning this king of black dusters. The wind has taken control, and spiraling dust devils bigger than the house are swirling about with hurricane force.

The house is rattling and shaking, and I fear we will be blown away! Ruth asked what we did to make God so angry. I told her we didn't do anything, and God's not angry. I assured her the storm will pass and everything will be fine, but I wonder. The blackness has arrived — I can't

Friday, April 19, 1935

I thought I could try to write, but all I can do is cry.

Sunday, April 21, 1935

Today is Easter, a day of celebrating a miracle.

It's a miracle that I am here to celebrate. Ruth and I survived the storm alone. Our prayers for God to protect us were answered.

Immediately after the storm, Daddy led a search party

of men to look for Ruth and me. When they found us in Helen's house, we were weak and unable to move, sitting in inches of thick heavy dirt with the then-black towel still over our noses and mouths.

Daddy and the men rushed us home and sent for the doctor. I couldn't understand why, until I began choking and coughing up dirt, and I found it getting harder to breathe.

Dr. Pritchard came and told Mama and Daddy we'd both breathed in a tremendous amount of dust and to watch carefully to see that it doesn't develop into dust pneumonia. With a smile and a wink, he said we'll do just fine because we're both strong, healthy girls, and he knows we'll be in good care since Mama used to be a nurse.

Mama was worried to pieces about us and kept a mixture of kerosene and lard rubbed on our throats and chests to help us breathe. It smelled awful, but neither of us dared to complain. For several days, Ruth and I coughed and spewed up dirt, and we still get short of breath if we do too much.

Monday, April 22, 1935

Ruth and I returned to school today for the first time since being stranded during the black duster. Everyone seemed a little kinder since we'd been so sick, except for Sadie, of course. She was green with envy, because Miss Boston commended Ruth and me in front of the entire class for our courage during the storm.

I nearly began crying again during noontime when Helen wasn't there to sit by me. Sadie boasted all morning about how wonderful her group's drama presentation is going to be. She loudly asked Betsy how on earth our group will still enter the contest without Helen. I can't even think about the End of School Festival now. School will never be the same.

Wednesday, April 24, 1935

When Daddy was in town today, he heard more stories of the awful duster. Folks near and far now fittingly refer to it as "Black Sunday," the worst storm anyone's yet to see. It spread its terror throughout Kansas, Oklahoma, Colorado, New Mexico, and the Texas Panhandle.

The darkness was like midnight, and cars were left abandoned on the highways and city streets as people tried to seek shelter. A man who lived not far from our farm tried to make it home from town in his car. The dust was so black and so blinding that he drove clear off the road and into the steep ditch. He was finally found several days later, buried and suffocated by the thick dust. His funeral was today.

Thursday, April 25, 1935

The four remaining members of our Dramatic Competition group stayed after school to discuss a practice schedule. As Miss Boston cleaned the blackboards, she overheard our concerns, and kindly suggested taking an hour during school several times each week to hold practices.

Betsy was a little agitated about losing so much practice time after Black Sunday, and she inadvertently spouted, "We're so far behind now since Helen moved and Grace was sick!" When she saw the look on my face, though, she immediately apologized, sheepishly remarking that she has a big mouth. I don't know if I even care anymore about the Dramatic Competition.

Friday, April 26, 1935

I miss Helen more than I can stand! I think of her every day. Dear Lord, help the Walkers reach California, find a job, and get back on their feet.

I mostly cough just at night now, and staying indoors is helping my lungs heal. Ruth was up and chattering away only a few days after the big duster — a sure sign she's in fine health.

Saturday, April 27, 1935

The Mayfields stopped by this evening to visit. Mr. and Mrs. Mayfield and Mama and Daddy drank coffee and talked a good long while about Black Sunday. According to Mr. Mayfield, the fiercely blowing dust created static electricity that was greater than anything this area's ever seen. A farmer south of Dalhart was only a short distance from his barn when the storm struck and he spent over an hour trying to find it in the thick blackness. He attempted to stay close to his horse, but the horse was so charged with static electricity that the man was nearly knocked down every time he touched the animal. Several folks who tried to make their way home in automobiles were stranded as the static electricity in the air shorted out their engines.

Before leaving, Mr. Mayfield said he has only twenty-five more acres to plow, and then he'll be ready to start planting. He told Daddy after that's all done, he'll bring his tractor over to our farm to help get the plowing started until Daddy's tractor is fixed. Daddy smiled and gratefully accepted the offer.

"That's what friends are for, Gilbert," Mr. Mayfield said as he patted Daddy on the back. "You and your family were an answer to our prayers when our roof collapsed."

Sunday, April 28, 1935

During the morning church service, I had a mild coughing bout; Ruth and I still have trouble with that every so often. At least my chest isn't aching sore anymore when I do cough. Mama seems to understand how I've been feeling lately, and let me have a little time to myself to take a walk.

When I walked over the hill a ways, I could see the Walkers' farm in the distance. It struck me how Helen's house had saved Ruth's and my life, and now it sits, desolate and empty, no one even making the effort to turn up the soil in the dry fields. The windmill only has two blades left. I guess Bud McCall hasn't found anyone willing to rent the place.

I miss Helen.

Monday, April 29, 1935

When Daddy stopped at Winchell's Feed and Seed this afternoon, he found out several more families are evacuating after Black Sunday — most say it was just the "last straw." Daddy told one discouraged farmer that our family would never even think of leaving the Panhandle. The man managed a slight smile and pointed to the headline of the newspaper he was holding. The front page of the *Dalhart Texan* featured an announcement:

THE LAST MAN CLUB IS OPEN FOR MEMBERSHIP TO THOSE CITIZENS OF THE PANHANDLE WHO HAVE FAITH IN THIS LAND AND WHO PLEDGE THEMSELVES TO BE THE LAST MAN TO EVER LEAVE. MEMBERSHIP OPEN FOR ONLY A SHORT TIME. SIGN UP NOW AT CITY HALL TO RECEIVE A STRIKING MEMBERSHIP CARD. THERE IS NO CHARGE FOR MEMBERSHIP AND NO CHARGE FOR DUES.

Daddy stopped by city hall to sign his name on the register, becoming an official member of the Last Man Club and pledging, *"Barring acts of God or unforeseen personal tragedy, or family illness, I pledge myself to be the LAST MAN to leave this country, to always be loyal to it, and to do my best to cooperate with other members of the Last Man Club in the years ahead."*

When Daddy came home, he had the biggest grin on his face I've seen in a long while. He explained that the group effort was started by John McCarty, the newspaper's editor, to keep up the spirits of the men who pledge to never leave their homes or abandon their dreams here in the Texas Panhandle.

After he finished telling us about his new membership, Mama just laughed and shook her head, saying that it wouldn't take an oath of honor or a Last Man Club to keep us forever in Texas. If I could, I would join also, because I will never leave Dalhart, Texas, either!

Just as Mama finished speaking, a hard wind hit; dust and tumbleweeds pelleted the windows. We went to the cellar for tonight. Daddy said he feels bad for the farmers trying to get plowing done — the wind is just about doing it for them!

Tuesday, April 30, 1935

Hallelujah! Daddy's tractor part came in at last! Mr. Jennings personally delivered it to the farm, and Daddy had the tractor fixed in fifteen minutes flat! As I write, he's plowing away and hoping to start planting the spring wheat in less than two weeks. I noticed on the way home from school that several farmers already started planting today, and I imagine that's got Daddy in a fluster.

Wednesday, May 1, 1935

Mama read in this afternoon's paper that Texas's own Governor Allred is the latest member of the Last Man Club. I asked what the members exactly plan on doing in the club, but she informed me that they won't really hold regular meetings. It's more of an "encouraging effort" by Mr. McCarty to keep up everyone's spirits.

Daddy didn't come in for supper tonight and ate his meal on the tractor while he continued plowing. When I climbed into bed just now, I could see through the bedroom curtains two little glowing circles of light, the tractor's headlights, barely visible through the mountains of swirling dust. Daddy says he has to get finished, even if it means working far into the night.

Thursday, May 2, 1935

I offered to milk the cows for Daddy since he's busy now with plowing and planting. He was pleased with the notion, since I did a good job last time I milked. Dandelion's nearly dry now, so she won't even need to be milked at all. She'll mostly stay in the pasture for the next month while she waits to give birth to her calf.

As I milked Rosie, her tail lazily swishing a couple of flies while she chomped her hay, I found myself spilling out my troubles. Her sweet expression seemed to say she understood my every word as I shared my frustrations over the play and, most importantly, my grief over losing Helen.

As I spoke, a tear and a sniffle escaped. Rosie nudged me gently with her spotted nose and let out a long, low *moooooo*. I wrapped my arms around her silky neck and gave her a quick hug before I headed back to the house with the milk buckets, my troubles left behind in the warm stillness of the barn.

Friday, May 3, 1935

It's very late; I shouldn't even be awake, but I just can't sleep. Mama and Daddy are in the kitchen talking, and they sound so serious. I can't tell for sure if they're talking about money. I wonder what's happening? What could be so urgent that Daddy would stop plowing and come in the house?

They've been talking for an hour, according to my bedside clock. It worries me when they have long, serious talks. I think I'll make a quick run outside to the privy to see if I can find out something — anything.

Nearly midnight

Mama, thankfully, didn't notice me walking past the doorway — I was as silent as I could have been, and the wind covered my footsteps. She and Daddy both looked as if they had a huge burden on their minds. I saw Mama looking down at the table and shaking her head. I could only catch part of what Daddy said as he raised his voice in frustration.

"With all the winter wheat withering from lack of moisture, we won't even have any to harvest now come June. You know that no wheat to harvest means no money. Unfortunately, Edna, it's our only remaining option."

What is our only remaining option? It must not be good. Daddy seldom speaks so sternly, especially to Mama.

Saturday, May 4, 1935

Before the crack of dawn this morning, Mr. Mayfield puttered up the road on his rickety tractor to help Daddy finish the plowing and begin planting. All day long the two of them plowed nonstop as if the world depended on it, and I suppose in a way for Daddy it does.

Monday, May 6, 1935

Daddy sold Rosie today. I now know what has been troubling him and Mama these past few days.

When Ruth found out we'd sold our sweet old red Holstein, she cried and cried — Rosie was Ruth's favorite cow; she'd named her as a newborn calf. Mama held her close and comforted her. I was stunned, and my head was spinning with questions: We only had two cows to begin with. How will we manage if something happens to

Dandelion? I immediately thought of Helen's family and how they didn't have milk, or cheese or butter, or cream, after their old cow died. When I asked Mama, she said we'd be in much worse shape without spring wheat than without milk.

The money Rosie brought will now help Daddy pay for the wheat seed he needs to plant. Daddy's adamant about not taking government help; he says he will stand on his own two feet and first do everything he possibly can before relying on Uncle Sam.

After supper was finished, all I wanted to do was sit on my bed and ponder everything that had happened. As I looked out my bedroom window and watched the dust swirling around the corners of the faded barn that now holds only one cow, I cried, too.

Tuesday, May 7, 1935

Ruth is one unending surprise — or maybe one unending mystery is more like it. Right away this morning, it was as if she didn't even remember or care about Rosie being gone. I will never understand how she can bounce from tears back to her carefree smiling self in no time at all. This evening, she immersed herself in a game of make-believe with the kittens, laughing and giggling as always.

While Ruth created fanciful tales, I slipped out to the pasture after supper to visit Dandelion. As I stroked her smooth brown Jersey face, she almost appeared to be crying with her big contented eyes and long lashes. I think it will take both of us a long while to get used to losing sweet, good-natured Rosie.

How can things change so much in one brief month? Helen leaving . . . terrifying Black Sunday . . . Ruth and me getting so sick . . . and now Rosie. The weight of it all seems ever-pressing.

Wednesday, May 8, 1935

Daddy and Mr. Mayfield began planting this afternoon. At suppertime, Mama, Ruth, and I joined both men out in the field for a quick meal. We even had butter for the cornbread, since Mr. Mayfield brought along a quart jar of milk and a pint of cream. When Mama thanked him, he just winked and said that Ruth and I need to keep drinking our milk to grow strong. Mr. Mayfield has the funniest mustache, which is very blond and very bushy, looking like heads of wheat growing under his nose.

At school today, Betsy, Mary, Abigail, and I had a tough time dividing Helen's part among the four of us. It's going to be hard to pull off the play without her strong acting ability; Helen was always the star of the show. Sadie makes a point to tell us almost daily that she doesn't see how we could *possibly* be ready for the End of School Festival. Finally, Betsy spouted back, "We'll show you, Sadie, and everyone else, too!"

All I wish is that Helen were still here! I miss her so much.

Thursday, May 9, 1935

I'm afraid we may lose Dandelion! She seems to have a form of dust pneumonia. It's so sad how she can't get up and coughs up dirt again and again. Daddy thinks she's grazed too close to the ground while trying to find grass or weed stubble. As a result, she's eaten more dirt than any cow ever should. Daddy said the veterinarian can't come until late tomorrow. I hope Dandelion makes it that long.

Friday, May 10, 1935

Dandelion made it through the night! Daddy and I checked on her as soon as daylight broke. She has a strong will to survive and even a look of determination in her eyes — like Daddy and all of the Last Man Club. Dr. Pierce will come this afternoon. Time to leave for school.

Bedtime

Ugh! I really didn't want to see what Dr. Pierce had to do to fix Dandelion. He put on a long glove and then skillfully cut a considerably large hole in her side. I stroked Dandelion's neck as Dr. Pierce began pulling out huge clumps of muddy dirt and sand. I don't see how one cow could manage to ingest so much dirt! He then carefully stitched Dandelion's stomach and hide back together, reminding me of the mending we so often have to do.

After cleaning his surgical tools and patting Dandelion on her backside, Dr. Pierce leaned against the fence post, his silver hair shining, and his friendly smile reminding me of his granddaughter Betsy's. He told us that such happenings are becoming alarmingly frequent in both cows and horses, and it's difficult to prevent.

Dr. Pierce said some farmers wouldn't call a veterinarian out no matter what. It's a good thing we did; Dandelion might have died. Thankfully, her unborn calf withstood the surgery. Dr. Pierce predicted it will take about a week for Dandelion to recover back to her old self and probably back to eating more dirt.

Saturday, May 11, 1935

First thing this morning, Daddy had Ruth and me haul hay, grain, and water out to Dandelion in the pasture. She won't be strong enough to get up for several days. She perked her head right up when she saw us coming.

After breakfast, Betsy, Abigail, and I walked together to Mary's house for play practice. We're stumped about what to do for our scenery. No one, it seems, has anything that could be used as a backdrop, or any extra paint or supplies. Two of the other groups already have beautifully painted scenery. Last year, our group created a background using an old tablecloth of Helen's, but this year no one seems to have much to spare. Surely *something* can be found.

Sunday, May 12, 1935

Mother's Day. Ruth and I decided to make the day as relaxing as possible for Mama. We quietly went in the kitchen before daylight to scramble eggs and make biscuits for breakfast, much to Mama's surprise when she awoke. Ruth said disappointedly that she wished we had wildflowers to give Mama.

The Sunday school teachers held a Mother's Day picnic following the morning service, and the weather was just right for being outside. We spread one of Mama's favorite quilts on a shady spot of the churchyard and enjoyed the hearty ham sandwiches Ruth and I had prepared yesterday.

The celebration soon ended when a duster slowly approaching in the distance forced everyone to hurry to the safety of their homes. Mrs. Mayfield nearly panicked, quickly handing little Hannah a dust mask before the duster even hit and rushing to their truck at full speed. Ruth saw the questioning look on Mama's face and remarked, "Hannah can't breathe much dust, you know. It makes her cough." Since she's the Mayfields' only child, I suspect they worry over her more than anything.

Monday, May 13, 1935

Daddy and Mr. Mayfield planted the last of the spring wheat this afternoon! The Mayfields joined us for supper to celebrate. Mama butchered a hen and made her delicious fried chicken, cream gravy, black-eyed peas, and biscuits. Mrs. Mayfield brought potato salad and a heavenly pecan pie. Mama had Ruth prepare deviled eggs while she and I fried the chicken in her largest cast-iron frying pan. Hannah stood on the step stool and made up a big pitcher of lemonade.

When we joined hands to say grace, Daddy thanked the Lord for friends like the Mayfields who see fit to help in

times of need. He also prayed for a gentle, soaking rain —
enough to settle the dust and calm the winds, and most of all
to give the newly planted seeds vital breath to sprout and
grow. Now that the plowing and planting's done, Daddy
and Mr. Mayfield don't have to rush back out on their tractors after supper — at least not until the harvest time in
July! After the meal, the grown-ups gathered on the porch
to play several rounds of dominoes, and Ruth and I took
Hannah out to the pasture to see Dandelion's large scar
where Dr. Pierce had operated.

Thursday, May 16, 1935

Glory be! Just as Ruth and I were putting away the supper dishes, the almost forgotten patter of heavy raindrops
sounded on the roof. We rushed out to the porch, and sure
enough, big wet raindrops were plopping onto the dusty
ground.

It seemed as if the drops stopped as suddenly as they
started, but Daddy said the rain gauge measured one-tenth
of an inch of moisture! I can't help but be more hopeful —
maybe the drought *will* end!

Surely Helen will send me a letter from California before too long. I eagerly await the mail's arrival every day,
hoping to hear from her.

Friday, May 17, 1935

Mama decided that today was the day to plant our spring vegetable garden. The wet sprinkles yesterday moistened the soil just enough to get Mama enthused. The wind was calm, so she retrieved her spade from the barn and began digging, sowing, and carefully watering the tiny seeds.

Ruth and I planted our own little rows: several watermelons and a few pumpkins. I truly hope the winds don't blow away our tiny seedlings; last year a great gust came and swept nearly half of them out of the ground. I'm looking forward to fresh vegetables this summer, and I'll be madder than a hornet if the wind and dust ruin our garden!

Mama's going to miss having a flower garden again this year. Not only do we have to continue to be sparing with our water supply, but Mama said flowers would never thrive under these kinds of conditions, so there's no use in trying.

Monday, May 20, 1935

I don't believe it! That Sadie McCall is just too big for her britches! She boasted endlessly today about her costume for the Dramatic Competition. Not only is Sadie wearing something brand-new, but her mother had it *specially made!*

Sadie then had the audacity to outright ask about my costume, but I told her that *our* group is keeping everything a secret. She smugly turned up her nose and waltzed away. That Sadie thinks she rules the roost. Money can't buy everything, and I hope one of these days I get to see Sadie McCall find that out the hard way!

At least our group did resolve our own costume dilemma: Mary's grandmother gave us a trunk filled with her old Victorian dresses — lacy and frilly! They will work just as well as any new costume. They aren't exactly the right style for the time period of our play, but we're lucky to have them!

Thursday, May 23, 1935

It's sprinkling again this evening, even harder than last time! As I walked here to the hayloft to think and write, I was more than glad to greet the raindrops, like big wet kisses from lovable Brownie. Daddy's spring wheat will be off to a good start now. It's an answer to prayer to see the farmers' fields and Mama's garden shooting up little hopeful green sprouts.

When Daddy went to town this afternoon to sell several dozen eggs, he stopped at the Piggly Wiggly to buy a quart of milk. Ruth and I rejoiced to have a glass of milk again with supper; I can't wait for Dandelion to have her calf so we can have fresh milk and butter again!

I can see from here that Daddy just stepped out on the porch with Ruth perched on his shoulders watching the drops of rain. He has a hopeful look on his face.

Friday, May 24, 1935

After supper, I went out to the pasture to bring Dandelion into the barn for the night. Daddy's careful to keep her from grazing too much so she doesn't wind up sand-packed like before.

I noticed our hay supply is slowly dwindling as I pitched some down from the hayloft to Dandelion in her pen. Daddy's lucky to even have hay to feed her; many farmers have none. I don't see how the McCalls can afford to feed all those horses of theirs. They are mostly for *show;* they don't do any real work. How do they have enough hay to feed them all?

Saturday, May 25, 1935

So much has happened today that I can hardly write fast enough! This morning, when I glanced out the kitchen window, I was amazed at what I saw. Hundreds of skinny, brown jackrabbits were rushing over the hill toward the house! I raced out to the barn to find Daddy and tell him about the rabbits.

At first, Daddy looked surprised. His expression soon turned to worry, though, as he picked up his shotgun and quickly darted outside. I followed him out of the barn and watched as he leaped into the truck and drove off quickly.

The jackrabbits were still streaming in one direction; it seemed as though the earth were moving as the brown, bony balls of fur scurried on their way. Ruth stood on the porch, her eyes wide open in amazement at the incredible sight of hundreds of rabbits.

"It's like 'The Tortoise and the Hare,' except there's just a bunch of hares!" she exclaimed as I climbed the porch steps and plopped down onto the creaky porch swing. I didn't respond; I just sat and watched as the last few jackrabbits quickly scampered off.

After a long while, Daddy still hadn't returned. Mama hollered out for Ruth and me to get busy finishing our chores, but Ruth could talk of nothing but the invasion of jackrabbits. Mama seemed edgy the rest of the morning, and I just kept thinking how young spring wheat and hundreds of jackrabbits aren't a good combination.

Daddy's back home!

Bedtime

When Daddy took off his boots and sat down in the comfortable old chair with his feet on the footstool, I knew a story was on its way. Ruth climbed in Daddy's lap to listen, and Mama, wiping her hands on her apron, hurried into the front room as well.

Daddy explained how jackrabbits have commonly swarmed through neighboring Oklahoma and Kansas, trying to escape the dusters and search for food, but never before had they invaded the Texas Panhandle. One lone jackrabbit can do little harm, but when hundreds group together, they eat everything in their path, especially the growing, tender wheat.

After hurriedly rounding up several farmers and warning them of the approaching danger, Daddy and the men headed with their guns to find the rabbits. The starving jackrabbits had stopped in one of the wheat fields and were quickly devouring everything in sight. The men aimed their shotguns and began shooting the jackrabbits by the dozen. The long-eared creatures dropped dead like flies.

Ruth gasped and told Daddy that it wasn't nice to kill the poor bunnies. Daddy gently told her that one thing had to die: either the farmers' wheat or the rabbits. I later overheard Daddy telling Mama this won't be the last time the men hold a "rabbit drive," as they call them. I shudder to think of this happening again.

We had rabbit stew tonight for supper, I could hardly eat a bite.

Sunday, May 26, 1935

I found a baby jackrabbit! It had somehow squeezed into the barn and made a little nest in Dandelion's hay. Daddy wondered if its mother maybe joined with the migrating rabbits yesterday, leaving the baby abandoned and confused. I wouldn't have even noticed it if Brownie hadn't sniffed it out and barked up a storm.

The little critter was huddled in the corner, and only as big as my fist. His ears seemed too big for his small head, and his bones showed. He didn't seem frightened by Brownie or me, and I carefully picked him up.

I brought him inside, and Ruth and even Mama took pity on the poor little rabbit. He was shaking, and his whiskers quivered along with the rest of his body. We gingerly set him on a small bed made from an old dish towel and moved him close to the warm cookstove. He's a lucky little rabbit — I guess Pumpkin was too busy with her kittens to find him first.

I'm surprised Mama's going to let us nurse him back to strength, but I think she has a soft spot in her heart for helpless animals. Daddy said it shouldn't take long to fatten him up and return him to the grasslands, where jackrabbits belong.

Monday, May 27, 1935

I don't think I'll ever be surprised again by anything Sadie McCall does!

She asked Miss Boston for special permission to bring her group's backdrop to school, even though the End of School Festival isn't until Saturday. It's a giant, three-paneled wooden background painted with trees and grass, streams, skies, and clouds in beautiful colors. It had to cost an awful lot to make, and knowing the McCalls, I just wonder if they paid someone to paint it!

Betsy, Abigail, Mary, and I were discouraged when we first saw the elaborate background. Mary optimistically concluded, though, that if Sadie's group has spent so much time and effort on scenery and costumes, then their script might not be very good. I'm more determined now than ever for our entry to pull through. We need to prove to Sadie that showy props don't win the Dramatic Competition.

Wednesday, May 29, 1935

Only two days of school now until the summer break, and Saturday is the End of School Festival! Miss Boston has allowed us to practice every day at school this week, since we completed our end-of-term exams last Friday.

The younger children, including Ruth and Hannah, aren't old enough to enter the Dramatic Competition, so they're working with Miss Boston to perform "The Three Little Pigs." They are very proud of their efforts. Ruth was a little pouty about her part in the skit — pig number two — until I pointed out that, after all, the pigs are the most important characters in the story.

The wind saw fit to blow too much this week. I hope it has stopped by Saturday; it would spoil the whole event if a duster blew in. The forceful wind has Daddy worrying about the spring wheat, which is just getting a good start above the ground. I heard him mumbling to himself that too much more wind like this will uproot the wheat for sure.

Yesterday, Daddy brought home a cardboard box from town to help keep our baby jackrabbit from roaming about, now that he's getting back some strength. Mama saved a bit of the cream Mrs. Mayfield sent for making butter to feed to the little rabbit. Ruth has christened him Peter Rabbit, from one of her favorite books.

Friday, May 31, 1935

This was officially the last day of my sixth-grade year. Miss Boston handed everyone their report cards as the school day came to a close. She instructed us to enjoy the summer break and said most of our families will be thankful to have more of our help on the farms.

Several of the girls, including Ruth and me, volunteered to stay afterward to help Miss Boston with tidying up the schoolhouse for the play tomorrow. The older boys worked outside cleaning up the schoolyard before the festival.

I'm getting more and more nervous about the Dramatic Competition tomorrow. I just hope I don't forget my lines, and I *especially* hope we win first place again this year!

Saturday, June 1, 1935

Our group didn't win; we didn't even place. We just plain lost. We remembered all our lines, and we didn't miss a cue, but we still lost. Worst of all, Sadie's group won.

Our play couldn't hold a candle to Sadie's sophisticated set and her group's rendition of "Cinderella." Naturally Sadie, with her chestnut hair curled into beautiful ringlets, and a dress to rival a queen's ball gown, played Cinderella. The other girls had parts as the stepsisters and fairy godmother, and Hugh, one of the oldest boys, made a "special appearance" as the prince. It made my stomach turn to watch it.

We presented our play directly after Sadie's. We did the best we've ever done, making our performance of *The Mayflower Adventure* seem almost real. But with our simple costumes and no background or scenery, I felt shabby and homespun next to Sadie's glimmering dress and elaborate set.

I don't hardly remember any of the other performances; I was nearly numb. I could tell Abigail and Mary were downhearted, too. Even Betsy, who was fit to be tied over it all, couldn't find something to say.

It wasn't a surprise to anyone when Sadie's group received first prize. One of the boys' groups was awarded second, and our group — with our little, simple play — got no award whatsoever.

I cried and cried after I got home; I can't bear to remember the look of triumph Sadie wore on her face. Mama, Daddy, and even Ruth tried to comfort me, but nothing can change the fact that we lost to Sadie. I'm almost glad Helen wasn't here; she would have been the most disappointed of us all.

Saturday, June 8, 1935

Ever since the Dramatic Competition, Ruth seems to be making an effort to cheer me up, seeing as how I've been a little downhearted lately. She's even volunteered to slop the hogs every evening, a chore I do *not* enjoy.

Knowing how disappointed I've been over Helen and now the Dramatic Competition, Ruth drew me a picture of the *Mayflower* sailing on the ocean — "To California," she said, "to visit Helen." I'm amazed that she's even aware of my feelings.

Tuesday, June 11, 1935

At last! A letter from Helen arrived in today's mail. It gives me something cheerful to put in my diary.

Tuesday, April 16, 1935

Dear Grace,

I am writing this letter on the way to California, I've lost track a long time ago of exactly where. I think we're still in New Mexico, but I can't be sure. I certainly hope California is as good as it's made out to be: Then the trip just might be worth it! Our old truck barely creeps along the road, and it's miserably hot. All three of my brothers are constantly grumbling about how hot and bored they are and how slow the ride is. I can't say that I blame them — it is terribly dull traveling.

We went through Albuquerque a while back. We had to stop at a filling station to gas the truck, and it felt so good to stand on my own two feet again. I used to think Albuquerque was such a looooong way from Dalhart, but according to Daddy it's not even a third of the way to California!

Mama's old mattress came toppling off the truck onto the road yesterday morning. Now Mama and Daddy have to sleep on a mattress with a tire track down the middle of it, since the car behind us ran over it! For the next hour, Leroy and Chester argued about who hadn't tied down the mattress tightly enough. It will certainly be a miracle to make it to California in one piece, much less with all of our belongings!

I already miss noontimes at school, sitting in the shade with you and Betsy and laughing over silly things. As soon as I can give you a mailing address, be sure to send me a nice, long letter. I think of you every single day, Grace!

Your forever friend,
Helen

P.S. You must excuse my shaky handwriting — did I mention that this trip is as bumpy as it is hot?

Helen's letter makes me smile. I'm so thankful Helen is well!

Thursday, June 13, 1935

After we ate noon dinner, Daddy gently let us know that it's come time to let our baby jackrabbit rejoin his friends in the wild. Daddy's right: Peter Rabbit *has* outgrown his box by the cookstove, and we now feed him bits of grass and hay rather than milk. Mama tells us that pretty soon he'll be hopping all over the kitchen (more than he presently does, anyway) if we don't let him get back to the wild where he belongs.

Friday, June 14, 1935

We gave Peter Rabbit an official send-off this morning before breakfast. Ruth collected a small bundle of dandelions, the jackrabbit's favorite food, which she solemnly presented to him. She tied a small yellow hair ribbon of hers around his foot as he fidgeted, "So he can always, always remember the Edwards family, and so we can tell him apart from the others."

I rolled my eyes, and Mama and Daddy tried to hold back their chuckles. Ruth finally let the poor animal loose in the pasture, where a small colony of jackrabbits make their home. She waved good-bye until he hopped out of sight into the nearest burrow.

As we ate our scrambled eggs and biscuits at breakfast, Ruth sternly instructed Daddy to *never, ever* kill a jackrabbit while on a rabbit drive if it has a yellow ribbon tied around its foot.

Sunday, June 16, 1935

The Mayfields invited us to join them for Sunday dinner after the morning service. As we drove down the dusty road to their farm, it was beautiful to see that the few surviving fields of spring wheat are now beginning to turn golden — a wonderful sight!

I can understand why Hannah has such a difficult time with her breathing: The Mayfields' farm seems to have accumulated twice the dirt and sand as ours, if that's even possible! Mounds of sandy dust are piled against the barn, fencerows, machinery — everything.

We helped Mrs. Mayfield prepare the small ham and canned string beans she brought up from the cellar. "All I've got to say is, this year's vegetable garden had best hang on through these rip-roaring winds! We're running low on just about everything I'd canned and preserved," she said as she climbed up the cellar steps and back into the daylight. "These hard times ain't getting no easier."

This evening before I went out to close up the chickens in the coop, I quickly peeked down into our cellar. What I saw discouraged me: Just like the Mayfields, our supply of canned goods is slowing dwindling. I guess I had never really paid much mind to it before. I can see now why Mama frets so much over our little vegetable garden and insists we faithfully keep the plants watered. How on earth would Mama and Daddy ever be able to manage buying *all* store-bought food?

Tuesday, June 18, 1935

Daddy received an odd letter in the mail. As I was carrying inside the letters and newspaper from the mailbox, I saw the corner of an envelope peeking out from the folds of the *Dalhart Texan*. It had an elaborate seal stamped in the corner where a return address belonged.

I pulled it out and quickly noticed that it was sent from the United States Department of Agriculture, which made me raise my eyebrows. I shoved it back and delivered the mail to Mama, who quietly opened the letter and showed its contents to Daddy. He read while slowly shaking his head. "We're not going to take any of President Roosevelt's help as long as I can prevent it, Edna. We will just have to make do with whatever this wheat crop brings."

Later, Mama explained to me that the letter told how the government is handing out relief commodities. She said it could solve a great deal of people's need for food and necessities — *if* they'll accept it. I have a hunch, though, that many farmers, like Daddy, won't take a handout from Uncle Sam unless their family is to the point of starving.

Thursday, June 20, 1935

Yesterday, when Daddy brought in Dandelion from the pasture, he could tell it was almost time for her to give birth to her calf. Early this morning, Daddy stepped into the barn to check on her and was greeted with the loud *moooos* of Dandelion's new baby calf! She'd had it all by herself during the night, and the new baby was shakily walking around the pen, bawling at the top of its lungs. It's the sweetest, smartest little calf I've ever seen! Just like Dandelion, her baby is shiny and a warm shade of brown, except the newborn has a small white spot on his forehead.

Ruth was most disappointed when she discovered that the calf isn't a heifer at all, but a little bull. At first, she insisted she would *not* think up a name for him, declaring a bull calf is good for nothing. I attempted to logically explain that a bull means one less cow to worry about milking! Ruth quickly perked up and began trying to decide exactly what the white spot on the calf's forehead resembled. No doubt by tomorrow, the little bull calf will have a fitting new name. Daddy didn't want us to bother him too much today, considering he's hardly born.

Friday, June 21, 1935

Dandelion's calf was officially named Yucca. Ruth explained in no simple terms how she'd devised the name: The soapweed yuccas and a very few dandelions are the only flowers left in the dried-out Texas Panhandle.

Mama announced to Ruth and me as we scrubbed the breakfast dishes that tomorrow our family will drive into town to tend to some errands and pick up several more bags of feed for Dandelion and the chickens. That is *wonderful* news: feed sacks, made of sturdy, printed cotton fabric, are perfect for making a new dress!

Mama said that we'll probably sew me a dress first; my other two are worn nearly to threads. Ruth bellyached plenty when Mama explained there's not always enough material from the feed sacks to make a second dress, and that Ruth still has several of my old dresses to grow into.

I've already decided how I want my dress to look: a

smart little Peter Pan collar with rounded corners, a long hemline (Mama lets me wear them a little longer every year), and hopefully a summery flowered print.

Saturday, June 22, 1935

I was lucky enough to find three feed sacks with the same pink flower print. So often, Mama ends up mixing two or three prints for our everyday dresses if there isn't enough matching feed sacks. My past three dresses have been this way.

Mama said we can start cutting out patterns first thing Monday morning. I just know this will be the loveliest dress I've ever had! When Mama and I have it finished, even Sadie, with all her store-bought clothes, will have to admit this dress is pretty enough to be from any shop in town!

How I wish Helen were here. She'd be just as pleased as I am about my new dress. Surely the Walkers have made it to California by now, and her daddy has found a well-paying job. I wonder if Helen would still be here in Dalhart if her Daddy would've had a mind to accept government relief? I reckon he might have been too proud, and certainly, by now, they won't need President Roosevelt's help in California!

Sunday, June 23, 1935

During Sunday school, Ruth overheard the older children discussing government relief being offered to all the area farmers. Sadie's two younger sisters, Sophie and Sally, reported in great detail what they figured President Roosevelt's plan was all about.

Ruth was bubbling over with questions to ask Mama and Daddy after church. Daddy patiently explained that it's simply a way of helping people along during these hard times. Every two weeks, things like fruit, meat, flour, and sugar will be handed out to those who sign up for the program.

Ruth then asked if President Roosevelt will be helping our family. Daddy firmly shook his head and said we'll stand on our own two feet as long as possible. Meanwhile, it's important for everyone to help one another the best they can.

Mama quickly jumped in to remind us that there *will* be folks we know who take relief to keep their families from going hungry, and that's *not* a shameful thing. Then Mama repeated one of her favorite adages about how it's not important how much money a person does or doesn't have, and it's not important whether one works as a farmer or is president of the United States. What *is* important is how we behave ourselves when no one's watching, and what we do with what we've been given. That's what really matters.

Monday, June 24, 1935

All morning, Mama and I stayed busy in the kitchen creating a pattern for my new dress. We measured, sketched, and snipped out pattern pieces using a few old newspapers. Ruth sat chattering at the table, until at last Mama suggested she carry out the dishpan water to the garden and then go visit Yucca and Dandelion. She skipped away, eager to carry out Mama's "good idea." We both breathed a sigh of relief when she left!

With the house peacefully quiet, we quickly finished designing the pattern. Mama approved of my suggestions for the dress, although she insisted that she'll have to help me a bit when I attempt to stitch the little Peter Pan collar.

Tuesday, June 25, 1935

A letter from Helen!

April 27, 1935

Dear Grace,

We made it! We made it all in one piece! There are so many stories I could tell you about our journey, but it'd take more stamps and paper than I have to spare.

California is so beautiful; it can't be put into words. Grace, do you know how odd it is to look out at the world from the tops of the mountains and see green, green, green, stretching on endlessly? I've never had such a thrill. I'd almost forgotten what fields of lush crops look like while in Dalhart and certainly after driving through the Mojave Desert! Driving through the desert was the worst part of the whole trip — we were praying that the truck could make it all the way through that empty land without overheating or running out of gas.

Now, after seeing this beautiful California land, every mile of every day was more than worth it all. First thing tomorrow morning, Daddy, Leroy, and Chester (both of whom have finally quit bellyaching) will look for a job in the fields.

Even though we are starting here with next to nothing, I'm just filled to the top with joy! I can't wait to see what tomorrow will bring.

I pray you and your family are well. I miss you so, so much, Grace! Is Sadie still mean and nasty? You've got to beat her in the play competition again, Grace. I'm so anxious to hear from you! As soon as I have a mailing address, I will send it to you.

Your forever friend,
Helen

Wednesday, June 26, 1935

I was curled up in the chair near the front door reading when a burly man stopped by early this morning. With a grim look on his face, he gruffly told Daddy there's to be another rabbit drive this evening. The more they talked, the more engrossed in my book I pretended to be.

Not another rabbit drive! I thought. It was what the man said next, though, that turned my blood cold: using shotguns to kill massive numbers of rabbits is getting too dangerous; a bystander might wind up shot or killed. So, from now, on, *clubs* will be used to *knock the rabbits in the head!* I was mortified and didn't even attempt to disguise the look of horror on my face.

As soon as Daddy shut the door, I asked if he would be going on today's rabbit drive. He sighed unhappily and nodded. "These jackrabbits are destroying the farmers' only means of survival. Something has to put a stop to all this, be it with clubs or shotguns."

It's all I can do to manage eating rabbit stew, no matter how hungry I may be. I'm almost tempted to think government relief would be better than eating jackrabbits!

Thursday, June 27, 1935

As soon as Ruth saw Daddy this morning, she spoke right up and worriedly asked him if he'd seen Peter Rabbit with his yellow ribbon on the rabbit drive. When Daddy said he hadn't, she smiled and said with satisfaction that Peter Rabbit must be taking very good care of himself and remembering to stay away from the farmers.

Daddy said he doubts he'll go on another rabbit drive. Using the clubs, he said, is just brutal, and besides, it's time to start the harvesting now, not be out chasing jackrabbits. By the time we sat down to eat the noon meal, everyone was plenty hungry, and Ruth didn't bother to question what kind of meat was in the stew. I made certain to dish up mostly vegetables in my bowl.

Between the dust that blows as hard as ever, the dry, empty sky, and those jackrabbits, I wonder how *any* spring wheat has made it to harvest.

Friday, June 28, 1935

The air is filled with hazy dust as Daddy, and every other farmer near and far, set out to harvest what remains of the spring wheat. Daddy optimistically told us at breakfast that he's aiming to harvest at least one-third of what he originally planted in May. Ruth looked surprised and started to comment that only one-third didn't seem like much, but I kicked her under the table before she finished her sentence.

Saturday, June 29, 1935

Mama and I lugged the heavy black treadle sewing machine from her bedroom and into the front room. I finished cutting out the pieces for my dress yesterday, and Mama had time to help me get started sewing it together. Ruth begged for some of the fabric scraps and stayed busy hand-stitching a little dress for Miss Annie.

I enjoy working with Mama's treadle sewing machine *much* more than mending by hand! I can already see the shape of the dress coming together from the work we did today. I just hope it fits right, or Ruth might be getting a new dress instead.

All evening long, I steadily sewed. The hum of the treadle nearly sang me to sleep, but I continued my work. I'm aiming to have it completed, collar and all, by next Sunday. That way I can make *sure* that Sadie sees it when I first wear it! Mama's taught me some very clever seamstress tricks, and she commented that no one would guess my dress started out as feed sacks.

In a way, wearing a dress I sewed myself is much more satisfying than going to town and purchasing one from a department store — at a very high price, I might add. When Daddy stepped in the house for a cup of coffee and saw my progress, he told me that it will be the most stunning dress in all of Dalhart. I hope it is!

Tuesday, July 2, 1935

No sewing today or yesterday. Between milking Dandelion both mornings and evenings so Daddy can harvest, and also doing extra chores for Mama, I've hardly had time to breathe!

Wednesday, July 3, 1935

Daddy already finished harvesting and hauling all the grain to the giant elevators in town. Harvest didn't take long this year, since the wind and drought had already taken care of most of the wheat. Always trying to look on the bright side, Daddy said he can at least enjoy Independence Day tomorrow without itching to get out on the tractor.

Every time I hear mention of the spring wheat, I can't help but think of dear, sweet Rosie. This is the wheat Rosie helped provide for us when Daddy sold her. Rosie brought us hope to make it another year.

Thursday, July 4, 1935

Happy Independence Day! The wind remained calm today — taking a break for the holiday I suppose. Ruth and I spent forever and a day figuring out suitable patriotic outfits. We finally settled on our matching red plaid dresses that had long ago become much too short to wear. We tied big bows in our hair using the pale blue satin hair ribbons that were a gift three Christmases ago.

Ruth painstakingly crafted silver stars from the remnants of several tinfoil wrappers. We gingerly tucked the tips of the stars into our curls that Mama styled especially for today. *Just like the Statue of Liberty*, I thought.

After checking our hair and dresses in Mama's full-length mirror, we made a grand entrance onto the porch to show Daddy. Putting down the newspaper, he smiled from ear to ear and said in his deep voice, "Well, did Lady Liberty and her sister decide to make a special appearance today?" I grinned, and Ruth, swelled with pride, held her head high for the rest of the day.

Making a curtsied exit, the two of us hurried back into the house to help Mama finish the special meal we customarily eat on Independence Day. Pork ribs, baked beans, and warm buttered cornbread. Truth be told, the ribs *were* a little dry and chewy, but could much better be expected from a hog older than the Depression itself? The entire house is still fragrant with the smells of the roasted meat and Mama's gooey cherry pie.

Bedtime

We lazily sat out on the porch drinking lemonade and visiting until dark. Soon the fireworks show in Dalhart filled the sky with every festive color imaginable. When the final explosion had long since faded, we trudged tiredly in to bed.

For a time today, it almost seemed like *before* — *before* the storms, *before* the dust, *before* the winds ruled our land.

Friday, July 5, 1935

Mama read in today's paper that dust pneumonia is taking a toll on a good number of people in our area. The Dalhart hospital is overwhelmed with patients, and there is an extreme shortage of nurses.

A long time ago, before she and Daddy were married, Mama attended nursing school and worked for two years in the surgery room at one of the large hospitals in Fort Worth. At supper this evening, Mama spoke up and said she'd like to hire on at the hospital for a few hours each week.

Daddy's face was thoughtful, and he didn't respond for a moment. Finally, he nodded and said he thought that not only would it help those suffering, but the extra money would be a help to our family. Daddy looked at me and added, "Grace, you could go along and volunteer your help, if they can use you." The notion caught me by surprise. I never imagined myself as a nurse's assistant.

Saturday, July 6, 1935

At last, I put the finishing touches on my dress. Mama found little buttons in her button box the same pink color as the flowered print. The Peter Pan collar even turned out without too much trouble. Mama and I did have to rip out the stitching once and resew it, but we hid it so well, no one will ever know. Mama showed me a fancy embroidery stitch called the daisy stitch to add to the collar, and I stitched little flowers on one of my hair ribbons to match.

Sunday, July 7, 1935

I wore my new dress to church this morning, and I held my head a little higher than usual when Sadie gawked and frowned. She couldn't even manage a nasty comment when Mary and Abigail hugged me and made a big fuss over my sewing ability! Ruth told me afterward that I looked by far prettier in my lovely new dress than Sadie does any old day.

A duster blew in just after we arrived at Sunday school. The boys and some of the braver girls, including Betsy, stood at the window and watched as the stormy cloud of churning red dust crept nearer. I stayed in my seat and looked at the floor. I had no desire whatsoever to watch a good deal of the Oklahoma Panhandle blow in.

According to Ruth, her Sunday school teacher prayed a very lengthy prayer, and when the younger children opened their eyes they shrieked, because the church was clouded in dust. Ruth secretly told me that *she* didn't scream when the prayer was over, because she'd peeked "to see what was happening." I didn't bother telling Mama, since she was already in a tizzy over the duster.

Monday, July 8, 1935

Ruth and I are quite proud of Mama's willingness and courage. Tomorrow will be her first official day as a nurse, and I'll begin going along with her after she's settled into her routine duties at the hospital.

Tonight Mama tried on her crisp white nurse's uniform and cap for us to see; she looks so wonderfully important and official. When Daddy stepped in and saw Mama modeling her uniform, he picked her up, twirled her around, and gave her a big kiss!

Tuesday, July 9, 1935

When Mama came home from the hospital this afternoon, she seemed a little sad but hopeful when I asked her to tell us about the patients. It's mostly children and the elderly who have been stricken with dust pneumonia, and they have a terrible time trying to breathe.

Mama said members of the Dalhart Red Cross have been busy making more dust masks for hospital patients. She also explained how the nurses and doctors each have assigned duties to carry out when a bad duster hits the hospital. Mama's responsibility is to put damp sheets over the windows and dust masks on patients in rooms 100–108 when a storm is approaching.

Mama said she's proud as a peacock of Ruth and me for "managing the household," as she calls it, while she was at the hospital. Surprisingly enough, Ruth and I hung out wash, hauled water to the garden, and fixed the noon meal by the time Daddy came in to eat. He didn't even utter a complaint when he tasted our cornbread. We figured it was best that he didn't know we had scraped off the burned part!

Thursday, July 11, 1935

This morning, I will set out to the hospital with Mama. I've never spent very long in a hospital ward, much less an entire day. What will I find there? In the bottom of my stomach a feeling is creeping up that I try to ignore. I worry I'll see someone I know who is sick. The very thought leaves me frightened.

Bedtime

As Daddy drove us to the hospital, Mama gently prepared me for what lay ahead. Many patients, she said, are quietly struggling to avoid the inevitable. Others are recovering rapidly.

Most of the day, I helped the patients who were able to swallow to eat their small meals. Sometimes I fetched water for a patient, which seemed to cause a chain reaction. As soon as one person's thirst was quenched, another would weakly ask for a drink. I took the pitcher from patient to patient, careful to not spill a drop.

There were only a few folks in the hospital that looked to be about Mama and Daddy's age, though I could never imagine my parents becoming that pale, thin, and out of breath. Mostly the patients are elderly, and there are quite a few children. The whole building is filled with coughing: loud hacking coughs, as well as mere echoes of coughs from those who are doing well to even be able to cough.

I spent nearly an hour rubbing the back of a small boy while his parents anxiously sat on a nearby vacant hospital bed. They had not budged since their baby had taken sick. I could see feelings so clearly in their eyes: fear, dread, worry, and a tiny strand of hope that had not been shattered.

Friday, July 12, 1935

Today when I returned to the hospital with Mama, I was anxious to see each of the patients again, but before Mama and I had even begun helping sort the morning medications, the parents of the little boy I had so carefully tended came rushing down the hall, tears in their eyes. I was startled — what had happened?

"He's . . . he's —" The child's mother couldn't put a sentence together, she was sobbing so hard. Along with at least half a dozen nurses, I hurried to the little boy's room. To our surprise and delight, he was sitting up in the rumpled sheets, rubbing his eyes with his plump little fist. A pouty look was on his face, and he looked on the verge of tears — it was the first sign that his fever had broken since he'd arrived at the hospital.

His mother raced across the room and wrapped him up in her arms, smothering him with kisses. His father looked ready to burst from happiness. By the end of the day, his thankful parents knew they would be taking him home soon.

Ruth keeps pestering me while I'm trying to write, wanting to know all about my day at the hospital. Mama's told her she's still too little to hear about all the goings-on in a hospital, but surely it can't hurt for her to hear about the little boy who recovered today. Maybe that will satisfy her curiosity. She thinks that a hospital can always make people feel better. If only that were true!

Saturday, July 13, 1935

Mama was up before the crack of dawn to start canning. Ruth and I trudged into the kitchen about daylight to help with the long day's work ahead. We picked, we washed, we cut, we boiled, and we put up in jars . . . endlessly. The kitchen stayed swelteringly hot. By noon, all three of us were sweating and hotter than a frying pan. Seems I wound up doing twice as much work as Ruth, who found it necessary to arrange string beans into letters and shapes.

When we finished for the day, we carried the canned goods down into the cool cellar and stood surveying our colorful results. Although we didn't anywhere near fill all the shelves, Mama said when all's said and done, we'll wind up putting up enough vegetables to last well through the winter. It really is a blessing that our little garden grew anything at all this year, and the jars do look pretty, neatly lined up in a rainbow of colors. Nevertheless, I'd much rather be at the hospital any day than in the steamy kitchen canning!

Monday, July 15, 1935

After breakfast and morning chores, I'm going to the hospital to help Mama. There aren't many big important things that I can do, but the nurses are still glad to have someone there to do the little things.

Evening

Mama let me take a break to eat the cornbread, beans, and sandwiches we'd packed, and I'm now sitting outside on the hospital steps, watching the hazy horizon. This morning an old, old man with dust pneumonia told me with a weak smile, "Don't you worry yourself none about all this dust and drought — why, today we's one day closer to it raining than we was yesterday!" Thinking about it, I reckon he's right!

Tuesday, July 16, 1935

A letter from Helen! I downright cried when I read of her new life in California.

May 15, 1935

Dear Grace,

We're living in a little camp with many other folks from the Texas and Oklahoma Panhandles. Just like us, they were let down by the exaggerations about California. It's become an unending, horrid camping trip: a shabby little tent to call home, campfires are the closest thing to a stove, and one privy for more than twenty of us to share. Daddy, Leroy, and Chester spend nearly all day searching for a job, but so far they haven't had any luck at all.

A week or so ago, Daddy found a job picking peaches for a day. It's ironic, isn't it — in this land of bountiful crops and green, green hills, the pickers aren't even allowed to eat any of the peaches, even though excess fruit is left lying on the ground to rot.

While Daddy was in the orchard picking peaches, he saw two little children of one of the women workers attempting to eat some of the leftover fruit. The orchard manager spotted them and bellowed at the top of his voice for them to "leave that fruit alone!!!" The

hungry children couldn't have been more than six
years old, Grace!

That's nothing compared with what Chester
saw happen in an orchard. While the whole field of
famished pickers looked on, the orchard manager poured
gasoline over a pile of perfectly edible peaches. He
tossed a match on it and walked away as it went up in
flames.

I cried when Chester told us, Grace. I just couldn't
help it. There are thousands of us next to starvation,
and food is being burned! It just doesn't make sense.

I finally have a mailing address, Grace, so you can
write me! I printed it on the back of the envelope for
you. I'm sorry it sometimes takes my letters so long to
reach you — often the envelope sits waiting for Daddy to
buy a postage stamp. Write me as soon as you can!

Your forever friend,
Helen

As soon as I finished reading Helen's news, I wrote her a
long, three-page letter, catching her up on all the happenings since she left. At least I now have a way to answer her!

Wednesday, July 17, 1935

I sat this afternoon at the side of an elderly wrinkled lady with snowy white hair, listening to her talk and keeping her company. She began telling me how years and years ago her newborn son was so tiny that he could fit into doll clothes. He was sickly, and it was a struggle to keep him alive. They even used an eyedropper to feed him and hot water bottles to keep him warm.

"Yes, we loved our baby Jimmy," she said with a misty smile. I could guess the sad ending, since I'd already heard familiar stories of babies and children dying from several of the elderly patients.

"Of course," the old woman added, her face brightening, "I guess he's not really our baby anymore — he turned seventy-four just last month."

I was taken completely by surprise and could hardly stammer a polite, "No, ma'am, I suppose he isn't." If I ever happen to meet "baby Jimmy," I know I'm going to burst into giggles!

Thursday, July 18, 1935

For the past couple days, many of the nurses at the hospital have been discussing the arrival of a respiratory doctor from

Fort Worth. He's been traveling throughout the rural areas that have been hit hardest by the dust storms, treating patients stricken with dust pneumonia. He arrived in his shiny new automobile at *our* hospital this afternoon, just as Mama and I were leaving. The hospital was a flurry of excitement as soon as word spread that Dr. Lambert is here.

No one had any idea that he would be stopping in Dalhart so soon, but it's a great relief now that he's here. He'll remain in town for more than two weeks, treating patients in and around Dalhart.

Friday, July 19, 1935

Nurse Wilcox, the head nurse, introduced Mama and me to Dr. Lambert. He's a funny-looking man, with a long, crooked nose but a smile as big as Texas.

I'm amazed how cheerful and happy Dr. Lambert can be, especially considering he deals with death and sickness every day. It's as if a fresh spring breeze has blown through the hospital with Dr. Lambert here, giving each worn patient and every tired nurse a reason to hope for the better. Mama said he's just the kind of physician the Texas Panhandle desperately needs.

Tuesday, July 23, 1935

I was more than ready for a strong wind to come and sweep me away this afternoon! I was on my way to assist Dr. Lambert and passed through the hospital ward with patients suffering from very severe cases of dust pneumonia. I noticed a boy, about my age, standing at a window. I was aghast; the patients aren't supposed to be out of bed at all. I firmly told the young man to please return to his bed, that walking about isn't allowed. He smiled and turned toward me, politely introducing himself.

He wasn't a patient, or even the relative of a patient: He was *Dr. Lambert's son*, David Lambert! My face was so hot, and I wanted nothing more than to run out of the room. He is quite handsome, and looks nothing like his father except for that same wide smile. His sparkling green eyes showed he was trying not to laugh, as I introduced myself and apologized bashfully.

He seemed enthusiastic to have someone his age to visit with, and I politely answered his questions about Dalhart. I soon remembered my promise to help Dr. Lambert, and quickly excused myself. I was *very* eager to leave the whole situation! Luckily, I didn't run into him the rest of the day.

Wednesday, July 24, 1935

While I sat on the back steps of the hospital eating my supper, David Lambert sat down next to me and struck up a conversation. I was surprised at how friendly and at ease he was, even after yesterday's embarrassing episode. He told me how he's lived all of his fourteen years in Fort Worth, a true city boy, and his father has been a doctor there as long as he can remember.

When I told David how I've lived my entire life on our farm, he was intrigued. I thought he was just being polite at first, but as we talked on, I realized he's truly interested in the way things are done on a Panhandle farm. It must be an entirely different world from the city life he's used to — he said he's never even lived in a house without running water, electricity, or a telephone!

It didn't take long at all for me to forget yesterday's embarrassment, and I soon found myself sharing stories and laughing with David as if I'd known him my whole life.

Friday, July 26, 1935

Daddy and Ruth drove to the hospital this evening to pick up Mama and me. Mama introduced Dr. Lambert and David to Daddy and Ruth. Daddy visited with Dr. Lambert

about the farm and then invited him and David to church services Sunday. Dr. Lambert seemed pleased to accept the in-
vitation, and the men shook hands. Just before I could close
the door to our dusty truck, David flashed his big grin and
said, "See you Sunday, Grace!" I noticed the wind ruffling
his dark brown hair as we drove away.

I couldn't help but smile to myself as we rumbled down
the dirt road on the way home, thinking about David. Mama
raised her eyebrows at my cheerfulness, but didn't ask any
questions. I'm looking forward to Sunday services more
than ever!

Saturday, July 27, 1935

We had an awful scare with a rattlesnake. Ruth went outside
to the privy before supper, and when she opened the door, a
coiled rattler was lying in the middle of the floor!

I heard her piercing shriek all the way inside the kitchen.
I nearly shrieked as loudly after I ran outside to see what
caused the ruckus. It was the ugliest rattlesnake I've ever
laid eyes on: Somehow, it had managed to stay fat while
most wildlife is scrawnier than ever.

Its rattle was constantly moving, and by the time Daddy
got there with the shotgun, it looked ready to strike. Ruth
has always feared finding a spider in the privy, and won't go

by herself after dark. Heaven knows what she'll do now that she's run into a rattlesnake!

We hightailed it back into the house before Daddy shot it — by no means did we want to see that snake blown into pieces. Daddy cut off the tail and gave us the rattle. Ruth set it on our bedroom bureau, making a beeline for it when she walks into the room. It sends chills up my spine every time she shakes it.

I suppose I can rest a little easier tonight knowing there's one less rattlesnake crawling about!

Sunday, July 28, 1935

I woke early this morning, brushed my hair until my head was sore, and immediately decided upon wearing my new pink flowered dress and matching hair ribbon. When I sat down for breakfast, Ruth — who had just rolled out of bed and looked like it — eyed me suspiciously. "It's not Easter Sunday, Grace! How come you're so prettied up?" she asked grumpily. I just shrugged, and she went on eating her bowl of cornbread and sweet milk.

By the time we had seated ourselves in church after Sunday school, David and Dr. Lambert were still nowhere to be seen. Just as Pastor Benson stepped up to the pulpit, they quietly entered the building and slipped into the empty seats next to Mama and Daddy. Peering around Mama's Sunday hat, David smiled at Ruth and me as the sermon began. I noticed Sadie and both of her sisters rudely staring from several rows ahead. I felt like a princess, seated so close to such a handsome prince.

Tuesday, July 30, 1935

I asked Mama if we could invite Dr. Lambert and David to supper tomorrow. She hesitated, and then agreed. My stomach is fluttering — I hope they'll accept! Mama said she'll be sure to ask Dr. Lambert first thing when we arrive at the hospital. It's time to leave now.

Evening

They're coming! I'm relieved; I had a tiny worry they might already have an engagement or, even worse, maybe not particularly care to come. David was standing with Dr. Lambert at the nurses' station when Mama invited them to supper. Right away, he flashed that breezy smile, and I could feel my face growing hot.

When we left the hospital, David called out that he's looking forward to supper and seeing our farm tomorrow evening. I'm not going to let Ruth help with any of the supper preparations — just in case. I want everything to be *perfect!*

Wednesday, July 31, 1935

Tonight was perfect! Mama butchered a hen this morning, and I helped her make chicken and dumplings. Mama was pleased she had enough fresh black-eyed peas ready to be picked in the garden, and I was pleased Ruth kept busy and out of the way shelling them. The house felt miserably hot with all of the cooking going on, and Mama commented she'd heard it was aiming to reach 100 degrees today.

When the Lamberts arrived, Daddy and Dr. Lambert talked nonstop. It seems that Dr. Lambert's grandparents used to farm, and he has fond memories of visiting them. My heart skipped a beat to learn the Lamberts happen to attend the same large church in Fort Worth as Granny and Granddaddy!

Thankfully, Ruth didn't have much to say while we ate. I'd thought to warn her ahead of time to stay quiet while the Lamberts were here. She did manage to boast that the sweet watermelon we ate for dessert was one she grew and tended in the garden. I almost added that it also was the *only* one we managed to grow this year.

After we ate, Mama poured cups of coffee, and the adults

moved into the much cooler front room for "grown-up discussions," as Ruth likes to call it. Ruth stayed with David and me and started to show him her beloved Miss Annie until I sent her a stern look. He smiled and asked if Ruth and I would show him the farm and all the livestock.

David and I talked about everything under the Texas sun as we leisurely walked around the farm, Ruth and Brownie following close behind. Ruth constantly interrupted to point out every possible thing she could think of. David seemed both amused and genuinely interested. He especially found the story of Dandelion's recent surgery fascinating.

When we arrived back at the house, Ruth disappeared to eat another slice of watermelon, while David and I sat on the porch steps visiting. He told me how he aims to be a doctor, just like his father. The Panhandle area has particularly captured his interest ever since he's been traveling with his father this summer. He said he might even return to this area to set up his practice someday seeing how there's such a need for rural physicians.

I told David how Mama loves her nursing duties at the hospital, and that I'm considering going to nursing school one day, too. With a look of sincerity, David told me that I'd make a wonderful nurse, since I seem to enjoy helping and comforting the patients. I was glad the sunset was by now turning everything hues of pink and red, or he surely would have seen me blush!

I also told David about Helen, explaining how much I miss her and how I fear I might never see her again. Letters are all we have left. I think he understood.

After the Lamberts left, Ruth wanted to know why David and I just sat talking so much instead of having fun. I told her to mind her own business, and she's been pouting ever since. I'm in too good of a mood now to really mind, though. What a wonderful evening it's been!

Thursday, August 1, 1935

Just as I was finishing my noon dinner at the hospital, David appeared and suggested we walk down to Denrock Avenue to Bell's Candy Shop. After asking permission from Mama (who gave me 5¢ and smiled when I told her where I was going), we walked down the hot sidewalks to the tiny corner shop. I don't get to visit Bell's very often, but when I do, I always make sure to buy a red-and-white-striped peppermint stick, my very favorite.

We sat on the street curb in the shade and talked nonstop while David munched on his caramels and I slowly savored my peppermint stick. It was fun to sit and talk as we watched the trucks and cars putter past. Mary and her mama drove by, honking and waving when they recognized us. I know if Helen were here, she'd like David just as much as I do.

Friday, August 2, 1935

A crotchety and complaining elderly man with a mild case of dust pneumonia was admitted to the hospital this afternoon. His grown daughter brought him in and seemed almost glad to have him out of the house. Now I can see why!

When David brought in the man's supper tray, he refused to eat anything. Nurse Wilcox had instructed me to be sure he cleaned his plate, which turned out to be quite a task. It took persuading from me, David, and finally the head nurse to convince the difficult man to even swallow a single bite!

Truth be told, I was relieved when he fell back asleep, even if it *was* before he finished the meal. Dr. Lambert predicted the man would be ready to return home by tomorrow as long as he agrees to rest and take his medication. I suspect that Dr. Lambert is as eager to see him go as the rest of us!

Saturday, August 3, 1935

Right on the front page of today's *Dalhart Texan* was a lengthy article about Dr. Lambert's temporary residency at the hospital. It told of his respiratory work throughout the area and how he's helped so many dust pneumonia victims. The best part, by far, was the handsome photograph of Dr. Lambert and David standing on the hospital steps. David had that same, big, sparkling smile. Using Mama's sewing scissors, I carefully cut out the photograph and article and tucked it in my diary. I wish I had an extra copy to send Helen!

Monday, August 5, 1935

Before leaving the hospital this evening, David invited me to walk to the library with him, if Mama wouldn't object. After thinking for a moment, Mama agreed and said she would pick me up at the library in half an hour.

David chose a historical book about the Civil War, while I found a large photography book about Prince Edward Island. Seated at a large table, we wound up whispering more than we read! David told me about living in Fort Worth, the high school he'll attend, and his best friend, Frank. His older sister will soon begin her third year of college in Waco, where she's studying journalism.

When I told David about one of Ruth's antics, it made him laugh until the stern librarian sent him a silencing look. I also told him how we've ridden the train twice to visit Granny and Granddaddy in Fort Worth. "There are always so many exciting things to do in the city," I whispered. David smiled and said he'll plan to show us the zoo in Forrest Park the next time we visit; Ruth would especially love that. Imagine, even after the Lamberts leave Dalhart, I'll have a chance to see David again!

Tuesday, August 6, 1935

I received the dismal news I'd been dreading. David informed me this morning that Dr. Lambert plans to leave tomorrow, moving on to Boise City, in the Oklahoma Panhandle. David's smile didn't seem as cheerful when he told me. He must have noticed my disappointed face, because he quickly changed the subject and told me a funny story, which he knew would make me laugh.

After supper tonight, Mama gave me a hug. She explained that I looked as if I needed a hug. I felt like I needed one, too.

Wednesday, August 7, 1935

The Lamberts left the hospital for the last time, just as Mama and I were leaving for home. As the four of us walked down the hospital steps, David jogged ahead to their car and returned with a small package. "This is for you, Grace. I know how much letters mean to you." He pushed the package into my hands before I could even think of something to say.

He returned to their automobile as Dr. Lambert started the engine. I waved until I thought my hand would fall off, and the last thing I could see was David's cheerful grin. I didn't open the package until Mama and I got in the truck to drive home. David had given me a box of blue-flowered stationery, with his address printed neatly on one of the envelopes. I'm trying to be happy, but I still feel as if I've lost one more friend.

Thursday, August 8, 1935

I wish I hadn't gone to the hospital today. I wasn't at all prepared for what happened. First thing this morning, when Mama and I entered a new patient's room, I immediately saw someone I least expected to be there. Mr. and Mrs. Mayfield were gathered around a hospital bed, and the hopeless, despairing looks on their faces told the whole story. Mama and I rushed over to them, and my stomach suddenly felt sick when I looked at the small patient lying under the stark white sheets: little Hannah Mayfield.

Mrs. Mayfield began to cry noiselessly as soon as she saw us. Early this morning, Dr. Pritchard diagnosed Hannah with dust pneumonia and advised them to get her to the hospital immediately. Mr. Mayfield explained in a quivering voice that Hannah had been sleeping for hours, and you could hear how difficult it must be for her to draw every breath. Mrs. Mayfield sobbed, "When she's awake, she's too weak to say more than a word or two."

I could see the pain and fear in her family's eyes, and it hurt me almost as if it were my own young sister in that hospital bed.

Friday, August 9, 1935

We haven't yet told Ruth about Hannah. I think Mama is trying hard to find a way to gently tell Ruth what will be the saddest, most heartbreaking news to have to give a little girl: Her dearest friend is in the hospital dying.

I've prayed again and again that Hannah won't die; that she's just terribly sick right now and in time will be smiling and giggling once more. I want it to be so, though my heart is telling me otherwise. Sweet Hannah never seemed to be able to handle the dust very well.

Bedtime

Hannah hasn't improved, and Ruth is beginning to suspect that something is wrong. This evening she climbed up onto the bed next to me where I sat looking out the window.

"What's the matter, Grace?" Ruth asked, a serious look on her face and concern in her eyes. "Does it make you sad to go to the hospital?"

"Sometimes," I replied, glad for a way out. Thankfully Mama hollered from the kitchen for Ruth to come help finish making the cornbread.

Surely Mama and Daddy are going to tell Ruth soon? We can't keep it from her much longer.

Saturday, August 10, 1935

I decided to write David a letter this afternoon after Ruth and I had finished washing the noon dinner dishes. I explained everything that's been happening at the hospital lately, and especially about Hannah.

Ruth walked into the bedroom and saw me writing on the flowered stationery. "Ohhh . . . ," she said, acting like she knew *exactly* what was going on. I didn't pay her any mind until she asked if I was writing David a love letter. I fussed at her, and sent her from the room.

I hope David doesn't think I'm forward to write so soon — he won't even be back to Fort Worth to read his mail until the end of the summer. I truly miss having someone like him and Helen to laugh and talk with. I hope he'll write back!

Sunday, August 11, 1935

My heart aches for Ruth. Last night Mama and Daddy let her know about Hannah. Mama carefully explained how Hannah is in the hospital and is very, very sick. Ruth anxiously asked if Hannah will be better soon.

Daddy pulled Ruth close to him and said quietly, "Hannah may not get better at all, honey."

"But if Hannah doesn't get better, what will happen to her?" Ruth cried.

Mama told Ruth, in a manner that couldn't have been kinder, how Hannah will go to heaven. Ruth flung her head into Daddy's arms and began to wail and sob uncontrollably. Mama's and my tears fell silently, and Daddy brushed his eyes with the back of his hand.

There were many prayers for Hannah and the Mayfields at

church this morning. In Ruth's Sunday school class, the little children made cards that Mama will deliver to Hannah at the hospital. Ruth was very quiet and on the verge of crying all day. Poor, poor, Ruth. Even more, I am heartbroken for the Mayfields. How will they ever cope with losing their only child?

Monday, August 12, 1935

Hannah is hanging on, though barely so. Mr. and Mrs. Mayfield spend every moment beside her bed. Mama quietly told me that constantly comforting Hannah is about all that can be done for her now.

The elderly lady who told me about her seventy-four-year-old son, Jimmy, died last night. Her son came to the hospital to thank the doctors and nurses for all we'd done. He said his mother always talked about "those nice, friendly nurses who were so pleasant to chat with." Laughter was far from my mind today when I finally got to meet "baby Jimmy."

If only Dr. Lambert were still in Dalhart treating patients. Mama commented that she's not sure if even he could help Hannah; her respiratory system has never been strong.

As we left the hospital this afternoon, Mama mentioned we might take Ruth to see Hannah tomorrow.

Tuesday, August 13, 1935

Daddy drove all of us to the hospital this morning. Ruth tightly clutched Miss Annie and timidly entered the room where Hannah lay on the crisp, white sheets. As we walked in, Ruth immediately grabbed on to my hand. Her blue eyes were wide, and she surveyed the room as though it were a sacred cathedral. Mrs. Mayfield smiled wearily. "I'm so glad to see y'all, and Ruth, I'm especially happy to see you and Miss Annie."

Ruth asked in a voice barely above a whisper if Hannah was awake. She wasn't; the little face dotted with freckles held a peaceful look of slumber as she rested against a stack of pillows. Hannah's own beloved doll was tucked lovingly in the sheets beside her.

We sat at Hannah's bedside for nearly twenty minutes, talking quietly with the Mayfields. When Daddy said it was time to leave, Ruth looked down and lovingly said, "Bye, Hannah. Wake up soon, because — because we — because our dolls have a tea party Saturday, remember?" Ruth's voice trembled, and everyone's tears overflowed silently as we left the room.

Wednesday, August 14, 1935

We've just gotten word this morning: Hannah has died.

Saturday, August 17, 1935

Hannah's funeral was today. As Pastor Benson and those attending stood by the tiny grave in the cemetery, the hot wind rattled and blew. It felt as if the whole bleak land of dust was mourning alongside the Mayfields. It has truly been a day of sorrow, and Ruth has cried in Mama's arms all day long.

Sunday, August 18, 1935

Our family took a small meal to the Mayfields this afternoon after morning services. As we got out of the truck, Mrs. Mayfield stepped out on the porch to greet us. She looked grateful to see the meal we had brought.

Mrs. Mayfield informed us matter-of-factly that they were in the middle of packing, so things weren't too tidy. We followed her into the house, which was nearly empty inside. Mr. Mayfield stepped in from the back door and joined us. "But *where* are y'all going?" Ruth anxiously asked. Mama might have shushed her if she hadn't been wondering the exact same thing herself.

"To California." Mrs. Mayfield sadly sighed, as her eyes filled with tears. "Hannah's death was the last straw."

Mr. Mayfield continued, "We want to start all over, somewhere we can smile again. California will give us hope again, instead of wishes — wishing it'd rain, wishing the dusters would end, wishing the wheat would survive."

This was another sad day of tearful good-byes. Good luck, dear Mayfields, and may you find hope instead of wishes wherever your journey ends.

Tuesday, August 20, 1935

Hannah's death has had a terrible effect on Ruth. This morning I found her sitting on our bed, holding Miss Annie, just staring. We've each lost our best friend, though in different ways.

Friday, August 23, 1935

A truckload of supplies was unloading down the street at city hall just as Mama and I were walking to the truck after our morning at the hospital. Earlier, I'd overheard several nurses discussing the expected arrival of government relief commodities for area folks. Once again, I felt grateful knowing our family's getting along without President Roosevelt's help, especially now with Mama's added wages.

Men were busy unloading bolts of fabric and boxes of shoes from the big truck as Mama and I drove past the building. Mama reminded me again that a family accepting help when it's truly needed is nothing to be ashamed of.

Two patients were discharged from the hospital today. The nurses and I were thankful to see them leave healthier than when they arrived.

Sunday, August 25, 1935

While Betsy and I waited after Sunday school to join our families for church, she discreetly whispered upsetting news. With a worried look on her face she informed me that the government relief that just arrived in town is handing out bolts of fabric *identical to my new dress!* The same pink flowers and all! I was just as shocked as Betsy, who doesn't mind outright letting others know that *her* family wouldn't depend on relief unless they were half starved, sick, or old.

Now I'm struggling with twinges of guilt for feeling

mortified at the thought of looking like a relief-farmer's daughter. *I don't even want to think of all the pink-flowered dresses in and around Dalhart that are being sewn.* I strongly considered not ever wearing my dress again until Mama told me I'd do no such thing after all the effort I put into making it. What a predicament!

Tuesday, August 27, 1935

The coyotes were howling away tonight. Their voices sounded like an eerie choir, singing a strange melody. Ruth was just about scared out of her wits — she's terrified of coyotes — so Mama took us out onto the porch to listen, explaining how howling and yapping are the coyotes' way of talking.

Daddy took Brownie with him into the barn to hush her from barking while he checked on the livestock. As we sat together on the porch swing, Ruth's eyes grew gigantic as the coyotes yowled at the night skies. Their songs seemed almost pretty, especially since everything else was peacefully silent. It was as if the whole Panhandle stopped for a moment to listen to the coyotes talking to one another.

Thursday, August 29, 1935

School is set to start September 2. Mama gently reminded me that tomorrow will be my last day to help at the hospital. My eyes pool with tears just writing this!

Mama said I might be able to help at the hospital now and then on Saturdays if it doesn't interfere with chores and such, but it won't be the same. Mama will still be tending patients in the mornings while Ruth and I are in school. I don't want to face another day of good-byes!

Friday, August 30, 1935

I wasn't the only one with tears in my eyes when I left the hospital this afternoon. A dear little boy I've been tending over the past several days had big tears slipping down his face as he hugged my neck tightly. I'd spent many hours reading storybooks to him while he's been recovering from meningitis.

Mama seemed to understand the way I felt and gave me some time to myself before supper, allowing my chores to be finished later. I think the patients have become dear to her, as well.

To lift my spirits, I offered to sit with Ruth in the hayloft and read aloud her favorite Peter Rabbit book. Maybe it comforted Ruth a little, too.

Saturday, August 31, 1935

Finally — good news! A letter from David came in the mail, and will now be safely hidden in my diary!

August 26, 1935

Dear Grace,

I'm glad you like the stationery. Now you'll have flowers, at least until the wildflowers bloom again in Dalhart.

When we arrived in Boise City after leaving Dalhart, a duster hit as we were trying to get out of the car; we thought we could beat it, but we sure didn't. It took us a great deal of effort to find our way to the door of the hospital! We were coughing terribly afterward.

My father and I are finally back home in Fort Worth, arriving yesterday afternoon. I was surprised to find your letter waiting on my bureau. It's good to be home and see Mother (and her good cooking!) again. By the way, I told her about the molasses cookies you brought to the hospital. She said that she'd love the recipe if you wouldn't mind sending it.

My father plans to look up your grandparents
Sunday morning at church. Now I know what it
means when people say "It's a small world!"

I'm sorry to learn about Ruth's friend Hannah. It
must be hard for a little girl like Ruth to understand —
she lost her best friend just like you did, in a way. How
is your friend out in California?

September's coming, and I'll soon be back in school.
I'm not looking forward to that *very much. What about*
you? A one-room schoolhouse has got to be more exciting
than attending a huge high school for the first time!

I always think of peaceful Dalhart now whenever
I'm in the busy city. I've never before seen a sunset or
nighttime stars that can even begin to compare with
those I saw in the Panhandle skies.

Don't get blown away by any of those dusters, Grace!

Your forever friend,
David

What an odd but wonderful coincidence! David signs his
letters exactly like Helen: *Your forever friend.*

Sunday, September 1, 1935

I'm madder than a wet hen at Sadie! Before morning services, Sadie very saucily commented on the "new pink relief fabric" I was wearing. Of course, she *knows* good and well it's not — but that wasn't even what made me the maddest! Just as Sadie was haughtily remarking how glad *she* is to not have to wear "handouts," I realized Ruby Adams was standing right behind us.

I know nearly for a fact that Ruby's family relies on government relief, and she looked embarrassed and hurt at the careless words as Sadie sauntered off. I wanted to apologize, but I knew that anything I could say would only humiliate Ruby more.

Monday, September 2, 1935

Ruth and I set off to the schoolhouse this morning. Today I am officially a seventh-grade student, and Ruth a second-grade student. Ruth didn't want to ever have to go to school again without Hannah being there, and told Mama so. Mama gave Ruth a hug and reminded her to be strong.

The emptied flour sack Mama gave us was brimming full with our new pencils, tablets, and ink. When I sat in my familiar desk as Miss Boston rang the morning bell, I missed

Helen terribly. Since I began my schooling seven years ago, Helen's always been there beside me on the first day of the new term. I wonder if she's starting school in California today, too? On days like this, California — and Helen — seems farther away than ever.

Some things never change, though — Sadie gave me the haughtiest look when she waltzed in wearing a stylish new dress. I just rolled my eyes: Another school year of Sadie will be next to impossible to endure without Helen.

Tuesday, September 3, 1935

There was a new little girl at school. At first, I didn't even notice her; she's so quiet and shy. Ruth immediately saw her and pointed her out to me. Miss Boston introduced her to the class as Lenora Henderson. She's the same age as Ruth, but looks much smaller and thinner. I noticed that her clothes, though clean and neat, were ill fitting and thread-bare, as if they had been handed down many times.

As soon as we were dismissed at noon, and, after a little prompting from me, Ruth went over and sat by Lenora. I could see Ruth was having a hard time trying to carry on a conversation with someone so shy. The girl never even lifted her eyes from her folded hands. Bless her heart, it must be hard making friends, being so bashful. Ruth did learn that Lenora recently moved here to live with her grandparents, the Hendersons, because both her mama and daddy died of dust pneumonia in Boise City. How very, very sad.

Wednesday, September 4, 1935

Tonight I could hear Ruth whimpering under the covers before she fell asleep. She misses Hannah so very much, especially since school's started back up. Whenever Hannah's name is mentioned, big tears gather in her eyes, and she sometimes becomes a little sniffly during recess.

When Helen moved to California, I felt as if I'd lost a very part of my heart, but at least she's still alive, and I can write her. Ruth has awoken and is sobbing in her pillow. I'm going to quit writing now and comfort her back to sleep.

Thursday, September 5, 1935

Miss Boston announced good news today: President Roosevelt has begun a nutrition program, just for schoolchildren. It will provide hot noon meals for all students at little or no cost. Miss Boston said we'll begin the meals on Monday, since a cookstove will be brought in on Saturday. The older students will take turns during morning recess each day to prepare the meals. The younger students will wash dishes and clean up after eating.

Tonight I asked Mama if eating the school's hot dinners is the same as accepting government relief. She explained how most schools all across the country will make use of the new government program to ensure children are getting enough to eat. Daddy said Ruth and I each will take 15¢ to Miss Boston weekly to pay for our hot meals, and we must be very mindful to not make mention of families who aren't able to pay.

Friday, September 6, 1935

Ruth sits with Lenora every day during noontime, but Lenora just won't hardly talk. I can tell this is starting to annoy Ruth, and I worry she'll soon lose all interest in befriending her.

Saturday, September 7, 1935

Mama surprised me this morning by taking me along with her to the hospital. I easily fell back into my routine from the summer. It was like coming home to friends, seeing the familiar faces of the doctors and nurses, as well as several long-term patients who remained hospitalized.

Monday, September 9, 1935

As soon as Miss Boston rang the morning recess bell, we set about making our first hot noon dinner in the newly set-up kitchen area of the schoolhouse. Betsy, Mary, and I prepared the beef stew, while two of the older girls made three pans of cornbread. The schoolhouse smelled wonderful the rest of the day.

We were in *hog heaven* to not have to fix the meal with Sadie, even though Miss Boston had her scheduled to help. Neither Sadie nor her sisters even attended school today. Betsy commented in her typically amusing manner, "It would come as no surprise to me if Sadie and her sisters don't know the first thing about cooking — or cleaning up afterward, for that matter! Mrs. McCall hires on a lady to do most of the cooking and cleaning." Ever since Helen moved to California, it seems as if Sadie wears a constant look of haughty triumph. Most days I can't decide if I would rather scream at her or dissolve in tears.

I haven't received a letter from Helen in what seems like a month of Sundays. Sometimes it feels like she's not even alive anymore. Oh, I wish like the world that I could see her again. Just yesterday I was thinking how Helen loved to laugh with such a delightful giggle, but even after searching my collection of memories, I still couldn't quite recall how it sounds.

Tuesday, September 10, 1935

Ruth has given up eating her noon dinner alone with Lenora. I think it's partially because the other little girls were beginning to taunt Ruth about sitting with someone who doesn't even talk. Naturally, Ruth returned to her usual group of friends after such an accusation. When I asked Ruth why she gave in to their teasing, she told me confidently that there's no need to put out effort that gets you nowhere. Mama wouldn't be pleased to catch wind of *that* manner of thinking!

Wednesday, September 11, 1935

Sadie and her sisters were still gone from school. Rarely have they ever missed more than one day at a time. Betsy looked every bit as relieved as I was to enjoy another day not having to contend with Sadie. And I suspect we weren't the only ones feeling this way. Ever since her father, Bud McCall, started shutting down all of his tenant farms and evicting families from their homes, there's been a sort of feared respect toward Sadie.

Friday, September 13, 1935

It appears Lenora has finally found at least one friend —
she's begun bringing a little homemade rag doll to school.
Each day at noon she takes the doll and amuses herself by
making up little stories to pass the time. I imagine this helps
take away the loneliness of not having someone to talk with.

The McCall girls have missed *five* days of school! Maybe
they have dust pneumonia?

Monday, September 16, 1935

Rumors are beginning to fly about the McCall family. First
thing this morning, before Miss Boston rang the school bell,
the McCalls' nearest neighbors, Tom and Joseph Randall,
told how no one's seen hide nor hair of any of the McCalls.
They're just — *gone.*

Mr. Randall is one of Bud McCall's top foremen, so he
and a couple of the other men went on over to the main
house to make sure everything was all right and see about
collecting their wages. No one answered their knocks, the
doors were locked, and the window curtains tightly pulled.
After investigating the horse barn, they discovered the
McCalls' prized horses were also missing.

Miss Boston's brother was one of the hired men who

went along, according to Tom and Joseph Randall. That would explain why Miss Boston has seemed preoccupied with her thoughts lately. Certainly the McCalls didn't go on vacation, but where could they have gone?

Tuesday, September 17, 1935

Things are not improving for Lenora Henderson. I think she must consider her rag doll her closest friend and confidant. She always seems content and happy when she's alone with her doll.

This noon, one of the rougher boys, looking for a way to create trouble, spotted Lenora and snatched her doll before she could stop him, waving it around in the air for all to see. Soon, an entire bunch of rowdy boys were taunting her. When Miss Boston rang the bell, Lenora picked up her doll from the ground where the boys had dropped it. Big tears streamed down her face. While trying to decide whether I should go talk to Lenora, Miss Boston sent me to the kitchen area to supervise the remaining dish washing and cleanup.

It almost brought tears to my own eyes to see Lenora at her desk again, tears still rolling down her face. Must those boys be so cruel to a friendless little girl?

Thursday, September 19, 1935

Understandably, Lenora hasn't brought her rag doll to school anymore. I can see the pain's still there when the younger boys turn to her for a source of amusement. They call her "Rag Girl with the Rag Doll." Ruth and the other little girls are at least now willing to stand up to the boys to defend Lenora, but so far, nothing they've said or done has made the taunting stop. Those rowdy rascals won't even listen to us older girls. Nearly every day now, Lenora has tears pooling in her eyes as she sits down at her desk after noontime.

Friday, September 20, 1935

While Ruth and I pushed against the wind walking home from school, Ruth began bellyaching about having to help wash the noon dishes today. She was just explaining how it *couldn't possibly* have been her turn again, when we spotted Daddy out on the tractor, plowing up the fields. In only a couple of weeks, it will be time again to plant the winter wheat.

As I sit here in the hayloft, I can see a few puffy clouds on the horizon. Maybe the rains *will* come again — Daddy says they have to return to the plains sooner or later. Come planting time, he always seems so optimistic with that renewed hope for "next year."

Saturday, September 21, 1935

Mama started sewing a new school dress for me. Trouble is, Daddy forgot to pay attention to the feed sacks when he bought them. The fabric is not in the least dainty or pretty, but, I reckon a new dress is a new dress all the same. I certainly hope *this* fabric doesn't become part of President Roosevelt's relief program!

At noon, Mama put aside her sewing and told us we'd take dinner to Daddy in the field so he could keep on with the plowing. We loaded up dinner and plodded through the rows of freshly tilled soil out to Daddy, who looked glad to see us. Mama laid down an old quilt, and we sat right down on the dusty, dry soil and ate, just like a picnic.

Sunday, September 22, 1935

At church this morning, everyone was concerned about an early morning fire at the Hendersons' — Lenora's grandparents! Their cookstove caught fire and exploded, immediately spreading the flames. The kitchen, and everything that was in it, was completely destroyed, but at least the fire was extinguished before it could consume the only other room of their small tenant house.

There were many prayers said for the Henderson family, and after services, a group of men, including Daddy, went to help repair the damage. Mr. Greeley, Mary's daddy, offered to bring the scrap wood he had from his blown-down barn to use for rebuilding the kitchen. The Ladies Auxiliary members organized meal and food donations to take to the family. Mama said our family could supply enough loaves of bread and cornbread to get the Hendersons through the week. Mostly, everyone is just thankful Lenora and her grandparents are safe and, if nothing else, they will still be able to sleep in their house.

Monday, September 23, 1935

Mama said Lenora's granddaddy came to the hospital this morning to have his burned arm rebandaged. It was injured when he attempted to put out the fire; Mr. Henderson will now have to have it treated and dressed at the hospital every day for at least a week.

As soon as Ruth and I arrived home from school, we had to hightail it to help Mama get the loaves of bread and pans of cornbread ready to take to Lenora's family. I kneaded so much bread dough, my fingers are still stiff, and it was flat out hotter than a frying pan being in the kitchen so long next to the cookstove. The bread and cornbread are finally baked and ready to go, the house smells heavenly, and I am thoroughly exhausted!

Bedtime

When we arrived at the Hendersons' small tenant farm, several other families from church were also arriving or leaving. Betsy and her mama were carefully carrying in several dozen eggs, and Mary's mama, Mrs. Greeley, was loaded with canned fruits and vegetables. Even the widow Yarborough had brought most of her dishes and pots and pans since she has no one left to cook for but herself.

While Mama and I helped Lenora's grandmother find a place in the cellar to put everything, Ruth held up Miss Annie and invited Lenora to play together with their dolls. Lenora immediately buried her head in her arms and began sobbing.

When Mrs. Henderson saw what had happened, she quietly explained to Ruth how Lenora had set her rag doll next to the cookstove "to keep her warm" shortly before it exploded and caught fire. Lenora has been lost without her rag doll. Mrs. Henderson said she plans to keep Lenora home from school for a while; it's been so much losing both of her folks and now her treasured doll.

Tuesday, September 24, 1935

This afternoon, I was finishing my arithmetic homework at the kitchen table when, out of the blue, Ruth rushed into the room and commented, with the oddest expression on her face, that Lenora must miss her rag doll very much. When I agreed with her, she made an unintelligible comment and quickly left. A short while later, I saw her in Daddy's chair, listlessly holding Miss Annie, while gazing out the front window.

Ruth hasn't seemed her usual self since Hannah died. She mopes around while doing her chores instead of inventing amusing ways to keep herself entertained. It's been a long, long while since I've seen her dance about the yard while hanging up wash or blow bubbles into the air instead of washing the dishes.

Bedtime

I discovered something wonderful! I walked into our bedroom this evening and found Ruth sitting on the bed, surrounded by fabric scraps and thread, holding Mama's scissors in her hand. When I asked what she was doing, she smiled and looked happier than I've seen her in weeks. She proudly explained how she was sewing a new doll for

Lenora Henderson, since hers burned in the fire. When I realized the "material" chosen to make the new doll was the white cloth of Ruth's outgrown nightdress, I had to stifle a giggle. Mama would be far from pleased to see that!

It touches my heart to see Ruth wanting to reach out and help someone in need. I offered to help, which was sorely needed, considering Ruth had no idea how to sew a doll! I showed her how to draw a little doll-shaped pattern, cut it out of the nightdress, and then hand-stitch it together. Ruth seems quite content that she's doing something important to help Lenora.

Thursday, September 26, 1935

How can it possibly be? Helen's latest letter is almost too strange to be true!

September 16, 1935

Dear Grace,

I'm sorry it's taken me so very long to write you again. I was ill for more than two weeks with dysentery, but I'm much better now. I received your three letters, which certainly brightened my day (with the exception of the news about dear Hannah Mayfield and the terrible

Black Duster that trapped you and Ruth in our old house. When I read those parts and how we lost the Dramatic Competition, I cried).

A nurse! I'm sure you and your mama are the best, and I think it's wonderful you are helping so many people. You are right: I do wish I could have met David Lambert! I'm glad that you now have two forever friends! I suppose school has started up again?

Here's the most incredible thing, Grace, which you may already know, but I'll tell you, anyway, just in case. The McCall family has moved here to California!! I just about dropped dead from surprise last night to find them living in our same migrant camp!

Mama and a couple of the other ladies went to help the McCalls get settled in their tent. Apparently, Bud McCall lost everything he owned to the bank in Dalhart. Everything! He couldn't even pay any wages to his hired hands, either. The McCalls just up and left for California without telling anyone, thinking they might have enough cash savings to buy a fruit or vegetable farm.

The most shocking part is that Mr. McCall abandoned Mrs. McCall and the three girls at a roadside café not far from here. Mrs. McCall thinks he's gone just outright insane, running off with what little they'd brought with them. A man at the café was kind enough to tell Mrs. McCall about the nearby *migrant camp; he gave her and the girls a ride out here in the back of his truck.*

Mrs. McCall is still in shock and said she has only $2 to her name. Even so, I'm going to avoid Sadie at all costs. I don't want to run into her in California any more than I did in Dalhart! It's beyond my understanding how Mama can even be civil to those McCalls, but, as usual, she said we all need to help one another the best we can. I just never thought I'd live to see the day when Sadie McCall would be forced down to the same level as everyone else — it's strange what these hard times have done to us all.

Your forever friend,
Helen

Evening

It's true! Daddy stopped in at the bank this afternoon, and was told by the disgruntled banker that the McCalls truly had lost everything, and not only were they the best customers of almost every business in town, but Bud McCall was one of the few people who could always pay cash. Until now, that is.

Mama just shook her head and reminded us that everyone is in one way or another affected by this drought and Depression. It leaves me with no excuse for complaining about doing without little things here and there.

Friday, September 27, 1935

Ruth and I finished stitching Lenora's doll today! We'd been working on it steadily for the past few days. This afternoon we added the finishing touches, two black button eyes we hope Mama won't miss from her button box, and brown yarn stitched on for hair. Ruth was more than proud of her accomplishment; however, she didn't rush to show Mama. Instead, she insisted that we keep it a secret just between us until we give it to Lenora. "It'll be better that way!" she explained.

Much to everyone's relief, especially Mama's, Ruth's forlorn mood has finally lifted; leaving behind once again the happy, playful little girl we've always known.

Saturday, September 28, 1935

Another letter from David!

Saturday, September 21, 1935

Dear Grace,

School's in full swing now. Football season is just starting, and I'm a running back for our team, the Pascal Panthers. If you ever visit your grandparents during football season, Grace, you should come watch us play — we're pretty good!

Thanks for sending the molasses cookie recipe with your last letter. Mother made them the weekend my sister left for college; they tasted almost *as good as they did in Dalhart.*

I'm not able to go along with Father to the hospital now, since I'm busy with school. Algebra and Latin are trying to get the best of me. You'll have to write and tell me how the patients are faring in Dalhart. Father said the latest medical update he received reported that dust pneumonia cases are still frequent.

Just yesterday, I was telling my friend Frank about the peaceful town of Dalhart and your family's farm. I almost couldn't convince him that I really did *climb to the top of your windmill!*

Your forever friend,
David

Sunday, September 29, 1935

The Hendersons, whom I've never known to attend church, came for both Sunday school and morning services. Ruth, beaming with happiness, sat next to Lenora during Sunday school. Many folks made a point to greet them and make sure they were welcomed. I overheard Mrs. Henderson say several times how grateful they were for all that has been done for them since the fire.

After services were over, Lenora's granddaddy told Daddy that they will leave the day after tomorrow for California. Just like so many others. It will be sad to see them go; it seems as if *everyone* is leaving, one family after another. If the dusters and drought keep up much longer and folks keep moving, I wonder if there will even be anything left of Dalhart!

Lord, help Lenora and her grandparents find what Mr. Mayfield desired . . . "hope, instead of wishes."

Monday, September 30, 1935

Mama had Ruth and me busy from the moment we arrived home after school. We hauled up load after load of canned goods, eggs, and salted pork from the cellar, packing a box of food for the Hendersons' long trip.

Right during all the hubbub in the kitchen, Ruth pulled me aside and asked if I could check the little rag doll "just in case she isn't ready to leave yet." I quickly glanced over the doll and assured Ruth she was fine. Then she skipped off to have the rag doll tell Miss Annie farewell without so much as a scolding from Mama for neglecting her unfinished work! It really isn't fair.

When we arrived to deliver the doll and the food box, the Hendersons were pretty near packed. They head to California early tomorrow morning. I hope with all my might that Lenora's granddaddy can find a job quickly upon their arrival. Ruth gave Lenora a big hug as we prepared to leave. Lenora, too shy to say anything, smiled and clutched her new doll tightly. As soon as we were safely in the truck, Ruth burst into sobs. Even Mama had tears gathering in the corners of her eyes.

Tuesday, October 1, 1935

Another letter from Helen so soon!

September 20, 1935

Dear Grace,
It's funny the way things are changing here in California. I'm beginning to actually pity Sadie and

the McCall family; since Mr. McCall ran off with all their belongings, they have even less than we do, Grace. Daddy and the boys got three days' work in a peach orchard, and Daddy bought a sack of beans and cornmeal with his meager wages. So last night when Mama cooked up a pot of beans, we invited the McCalls to eat supper with us.

Sadie's little sister Sophie quietly said that they would have gone without eating that day if we hadn't shared with them. I never thought I'd live to see the day when the Walker family would have more than the McCalls! I can't help but feel extra sorry for them, especially now that they don't have a daddy. Sadie even managed to smile and gratefully say thank you when I served her a bowlful of beans.

The thing that made me pity Sadie the very most is what happened here in the camp just yesterday when she and her mama tried to hire on to pick cotton. The vulgar and disrespectful field managers who come here looking to hire on workers laughed and mocked Mrs. McCall and Sadie. They could easily see neither one had ever done much labor, by the looks of their hands and clothes. I heard them rudely yelling at Sadie and her mama, calling them "dumb Okies" and "fruit tramps." They also said some words that made me want to plug my ears. Sadie ran back to their tent, and I could hear her crying late into the day (you can hear every word that's said within these thin, shabby tents).

*Sadie said she won't be continuing on with her
schooling now, since both she and her mama will have
to bring in some kind of wages. Daddy and Mama
can't decide whether to even bother putting us in school
here. More and more people call us Okies and yell
hateful things when we go into town. We're not even
from Oklahoma!*

*I miss Dalhart, and I more than anything miss our
long chats. Write me soon, Grace!*

*Your forever friend,
Helen*

*P.S. I'm able to mail off this letter to you right
away — Sadie brought a small roll of postage stamps
with her from Dalhart, and she was kind enough to
offer me one.*

Wednesday, October 2, 1935

I stumbled across the most amazing thing! As I was making
up the bed this morning, I reached far under the quilts for
Ruth's doll to place on top of the pillows. What I found
wasn't Ruth's cherished Miss Annie with the beautiful dress,
but, instead, the rag doll she'd made for Lenora!

Right away, I went in the kitchen and found Ruth

singing to herself in the mirror as she was washing her face at the washbasin. When I asked her to explain, she said, trying not to cry, that she'd decided to give Miss Annie to Lenora and keep the rag doll herself.

This is one of the kindest, most unselfish acts I've ever seen from Ruth. Miss Annie was her beloved friend, and I'm sure it was like giving away a part of herself. I told Ruth that now Lenora will give Miss Annie every bit as much love as she did.

Ruth and I did the wash this afternoon after school, and quite by accident, a very odd-looking nightdress wound up on the clothesline! We had to hurriedly take it down before Mama could spot the cutout holes and start asking questions.

Thursday, October 3, 1935

Ruth chattered all the way home from school about the new picture showing at the Mission Theatre: *Bright Eyes*, with Shirley Temple. She's been wanting Daddy something awful to go see it. Ruth and her friends have been crazy about Shirley Temple lately, even though Ruth's only seen one of her movies.

I'm not counting on Mama and Daddy agreeing with such a notion; it's been a long while now since we've gone to the picture show. Even though Ruth's carrying on is annoying, I wouldn't mind seeing *Bright Eyes* myself.

Friday, October 4, 1935

Another letter from dear, sweet Helen!

September 23, 1935

Dear Grace,

I have a good deal of time for letter writing now. With Daddy and the boys getting occasional work, I can buy a few postage stamps to send you more letters!

I've been talking with Sadie more and more lately (she's the only girl our age, really). You would be just shocked to see how different she is from the long-ago days when she spilled my inkwell. Grace, she even apologized for being so horrible to us all those years! What's more, Sadie confessed that she'd always been a little envious because you and I are such good friends, and both of us are smart and treat others nicely.

I know if you were here you'd think just as I do: The McCalls' financial loss wasn't such a bad thing after all. How else could Sadie have made a dramatic change for the better? We can only pray her scoundrel father will see the errors of his ways.

Daddy and the older boys are still working two or

three days a week. They're lucky to have any work at all, and we seem to be making do. I'm learning more and more to ignore the mean things people say because they think we're "Okies." I miss Dalhart. Write me all you can, Grace!

Your forever friend,
Helen

Saturday, October 5, 1935

Ruth turned eight today. Mama and Daddy surprised her this morning with two tickets to *Bright Eyes*. Ruth squealed and jumped around the kitchen, excited to see Shirley Temple.

Daddy and Ruth left right after supper to ensure the best seats. Ruth giggled when she saw Daddy all dressed up as if it were Sunday morning church services — he told her he wanted to look spiffy to take his special birthday girl to town. I secretly gave Daddy the 10¢ that I'd been saving for nearly six months and told him to surprise Ruth with popcorn and a root beer at the show. Mama and I made a special cake while Ruth and Daddy were gone. It was a fluffy golden angel food cake covered in silky white frosting made from Dandelion's rich cream. The whole house smelled heavenly.

Ruth returned home glowing from head to toe and explained in great detail the movie's entire story line as we ate slices of the cake. We laughed when she and Daddy sang "On the Good Ship Lollipop." Ruth sighed as we plopped in bed tonight and confided that this was the very best birthday she's ever had.

I smiled when she said that — we had all been a little worried she'd be disappointed. She didn't have a pile of presents like she's had in years past, but she was thrilled nonetheless with her special day. I guess Ruth is growing up at last!

Monday, October 7, 1935

A letter with handwriting I didn't recognize came in the mail for me today. I nearly dropped it as I read:

September 26, 1935

Dear Grace,

I've thought about you many times since I left Dalhart. Helen's mama says that hard times aren't so bad, as long as you learn a lesson from them. And I have.

Things are much different in California. When I encountered Helen here at the migrant camp, I expected her to be just as nasty to me as I always was to you both.

*But, having a heart of gold, she treated me like we'd
always been friends. Helen didn't taunt me because my
father left us penniless, or laugh when my hair was
nearly completely cut off because of head lice. She
even gave me her hat to wear, the one with the sage
green ribbon.*

*I'm ashamed of how terrible I was to you and
Helen, and hope you'll forgive me. You never returned
cruelty, even though I was deserving. I remember Pastor
Benson once saying that true happiness never comes
from the unhappiness of others. Maybe someday we
could be friends — I'd like that very much.*

*Yours truly,
Sadie McCall*

Goodness gracious, I have so much to think about! How on
earth can this be the same Sadie McCall that I always knew?

Tuesday, October 8, 1935

I don't know what to write to Sadie. It's difficult to just up
and forgive someone who was so unkind for years and
years. I know Helen was able, but she's always had a gift for
loving and seeing the good in everyone — and now that includes Sadie.

Wednesday, October 9, 1935

I stayed up long after bedtime last night writing and crumpling letters to Sadie. Here is the letter I finally decided to send:

> *Dear Sadie,*
>
> *I've learned my share of lessons, too, from these times we're living through. And I forgive you — after all, it's much better to have friends than enemies, isn't it? I would never have believed I'd say this, but I'm glad we can now be friends.*
>
> *I'm sending you my favorite book,* Anne of Green Gables, *to brighten up the days in California. I know you'll like it.*
>
> *Your forever friend,*
> *Grace*
>
> *P.S. Give Helen a warm hug for me!*

Thursday, October 10, 1935

Daddy whistled cheerfully when he came in for breakfast. He announced that he'll start planting today. With a confident and determined look on his face, he declared that it will be good to get the winter wheat in the ground, and surely, by next year, the drought will be behind us.

There were those words again: *next year.* So many folks seem to have forever given up on "next year." I'm thankful Daddy, Mama, Ruth, and I still have our farm, our family, and hope . . . hope for next year, instead of wishes.

Epilogue

Despite the Edwards' hopes, "next year" brought continued drought. In fact, four more agonizing years of drought and dust followed before the skies finally opened with precious rain, and the bountiful wheat harvests returned. As he'd promised, Daddy saw to it that Mama and the girls each had a store-bought dress, their first in nearly eight years.

In the spring of 1940, the Panhandle wildflowers bloomed once again. After carefully pressing her favorites, Grace included them in her next letters to Helen, David, and Sadie. Grace continued to volunteer countless hours at Dalhart Hospital before graduating from the one-room schoolhouse. Pursuing her dream of nursing, Grace attended Harris School of Nursing in Fort Worth. Shortly before David Lambert graduated from Baylor College of Medicine, he presented Grace a bouquet of wildflowers, asking her to be his wife. With World War II at its height, the newlyweds immediately enlisted in the U.S. Army

Medical Corps and served side by side at military hospitals throughout England and France.

After the war, David and Grace returned to the Texas Panhandle, where they set up a small medical practice in Amarillo. Inspired by his father, David spent much of his time traveling to provide medical care throughout rural areas of the Panhandle. After raising their four children, Grace devoted herself to heading the Amarillo Red Cross. Shortly after Dr. David Lambert's retirement at age seventy-four, he and Grace moved to Dalhart, where they built a home on the same hill where the Edwards' original house once stood.

Ruth Edwards completed her final two years of education at Dalhart High School, since most of the rural schoolhouses were then closed. She attended Southwest Texas State Teachers' College in San Marcos, and after graduation taught high school literature in Austin. Ruth married Clyde Drummond, an aspiring concert pianist who later conducted the Austin Symphony. Still every bit as imaginative, Ruth wrote a series of popular children's books, launching her lifelong writing career. Ruth and Clyde raised two daughters in a home filled with literature and music.

Gilbert and Edna Edwards (Daddy and Mama) were among the first farmers in Dalhart to follow the government's new Soil Conservation Program, helping to prevent further loss of the valuable topsoil. Mama continued part-time nursing, and during the war she helped make thousands of surgical dressings. Edna and Gilbert never left their beloved farm, but they frequently traveled to visit their daughters and grandchildren.

In California, the McCall and Walker families struggled to survive the harshest of conditions in the squatter's migrant camp. Sadie's mother contracted tuberculosis, a constant threat among such unsanitary conditions. After two years of barely subsisting, both families were finally eligible to move to Sunset Labor Camp, a well-run government facility. The families remained close and lived as neighbors in tents #249 and #251.

After the death of Mrs. McCall, Sadie was left to care for her younger sisters. Following her mother's example of determination, Sadie proposed an arrangement with a local grocer to operate a "soda pop truck" in the fields and orchards, selling refreshments to the field hands. Sadie was a remarkably clever businesswoman, and she soon caught the attention of the grocer's eldest son, Roger Fisher. After marrying, they opened a small grocery in Bakersfield, and by 1950, Sadie and Roger owned a chain of supermarkets throughout southern California. Roger was tragically killed in the 1952 earthquake, leaving Sadie to manage the business alone. Sadie had no children and never remarried.

After moving to the government-run migrant camp, Helen continued her education. She graduated valedictorian and received a full scholarship to attend Bakersfield College. Helen then taught at Arvin Federal Emergency School (Weedpatch School), a school established especially for migrant children. No one understood their heartache more than Helen. In 1946, Helen married John Bryan, a Kansas migrant she had first met at one of the camp's Saturday night dances. They built a small dairy in Tulare County, California, where they raised a daughter and two sons.

In September 2001, the one-hundred-year-old town of Dalhart celebrated its centennial. Grace invited Ruth and Clyde to attend, as well as the many children and grandchildren. Perhaps most fitting of all, Grace welcomed home Helen and Sadie, her forever friends.

Life in America
in 1935

Historical Note

The Dust Bowl era lasted from 1931 to 1939 and is considered one of the greatest ecological disasters in U.S. history. It covered a five-state area, with Dalhart, Texas, located near the center. Suffering through the Great Depression, drought, and severe dust storms for nearly a decade, many farm families lost an entire way of life.

The beginnings of the Dust Bowl occurred years before the rains stopped. During World War I (1916–1918), when wheat was in high demand, out-of-state farmers were lured to the Great Plains region to farm. More than five million acres of grasslands were plowed, producing great harvests of wheat that helped to feed civilians and soldiers overseas. Unfortunately, it was also setting up the Great Plains for one of America's worst environmental catastrophes.

After the war ended, wheat prices steadily fell. Farmers planted even more acres of wheat to compensate for the poor profits. Many farmers began using tractors, but while the tractor allowed them to farm more acres of land, it only created more financial burdens. An even greater problem than the amount of land being plowed were the careless farming methods most farmers practiced: They tended to ignore the contour of the land and burned the wheat stubble after harvest. It was only a matter of time until the topsoil would no longer stay where it was intended to be.

Most farm families needed little money to survive, since they milked their own cows, raised chickens and hogs, grew grain and hay for their cattle, and canned vegetables from their gardens. However, farmers who borrowed money from the bank to buy seed or machinery found it almost impossible to keep up with their payments without a successful wheat crop. Tenant farmers had difficulty paying their rent. By the 1930s, more than fifty-three percent of the farms in the Texas Panhandle were owned by absentee landowners and run by tenant farmers.

The Great Depression began in 1929, but in the summer of 1931 an even more disastrous misfortune struck farmers in the Great Plains. Wheat prices dropped further, from 50¢ per bushel to only 20¢ per bushel. Even worse, the rains stopped — and the typically strong winds continued to blow. Although an occasional dust storm was not uncommon, the Great Plains would experience them with a frequency and severity as never before.

When the first black "dusters" hit, some were terrified that the end of the world had arrived. The dust storms were powerful and forcefully blew stinging, blinding dirt, sand, and debris across the land. Often spotted as far as twenty to thirty miles in the distance, dusters were sometimes mistaken to be clouds of dark smoke or approaching rain clouds. Farmers continued to plow the dry, arid fields, holding out hope for a wheat harvest despite the drought conditions. In the spring of 1935, parts of the Oklahoma and Texas panhandles saw as much as eighty percent of the wheat acreage destroyed by winds. The Amarillo, Texas, weather bureau reported 192 dust storms from the period of 1933 to 1936, and as much as 850 million tons of topsoil from the Great Plains had blown away. Some believed they could tell where a storm had originated by the color of the dust: Kansas produced black dusters; red storms were from Oklahoma; and the dusters from New Mexico and Colorado were gray.

The worst duster struck on April 14, 1935, known as "Black Sunday." The day had been unusually beautiful, clear, and warm, with hints of summer. Many people were enjoying the outdoors when a low line of heavy clouds to the north began quickly moving in. The temperature rapidly dropped, and huge flocks of birds flew ahead of the coming storm. When the wind hit, the Dalhart area was plunged into darkness for over an hour before there was any visibility. The "black blizzard" made it impossible for drivers to see the road, and many abandoned their vehicles in the middle of streets and highways.

When President Franklin D. Roosevelt took office in 1933, he began taking measures to help end the worsening conditions for farm families in the Great Plains. One of the most important programs established, the Soil Conservation Service, taught essential farming techniques to help prevent further damage to the land. Farmers were paid to use these new soil-conserving practices, and by 1938 soil loss was reduced by sixty-five percent, even though the drought continued.

Most residents of the Great Plains were determined to stay on their land despite the drought and dust storms, but many families, especially tenant farmers, were forced to abandon their farms. Advertisements appeared that promised thousands of available jobs in California's lush orchards and fields. About one million people journeyed from the Great Plains to California — the largest migration of American people in history. Left behind were ten thousand abandoned houses and nine million acres of deserted farmland.

Upon arriving in California's southern San Joaquin Valley, Dust Bowl migrants discovered the truth: The large, corporate-owned farms had falsely advertised for more workers than were needed and offered to pay only extremely low wages. California residents did not welcome the large numbers of people flooding into their state, and often called any migrant an "Okie." With little or no work, many of the migrant families had no choice but to live in farm-labor camps. These "squatter communities" were unsanitary and disease-ridden, with crude tents and shacks made out of cardboard or tin. In 1936, the Farm Security Administration helped establish new, improved migrant labor camps. They provided hot showers, toilets, meals, and even a school especially for migrant children. Many families were finally able to find the hope for the better life they had traveled so far to achieve.

In the Great Plains, the long-awaited rains arrived in the fall of 1939. The "Dirty Thirties" soon became a memory. When the United States entered World War II, the country began its recovery from the Great Depression, and feeding troops overseas generated a new demand for wheat.

Today, Dallam County, in the northwest Texas Panhandle, is the leading producer of corn and wheat in the state. Farmers have restored the Great Plains to an abundant and prosperous land through conservation methods, irrigation, and a determination never to repeat the mistakes of the Dust Bowl era.

In the top photograph, taken in 1937, the black cloud of a duster sweeps over buildings and a parking lot, filling the air with sand and dirt and blocking out the sunlight. Below, sand from a duster has blocked the entryway into a farmhouse.

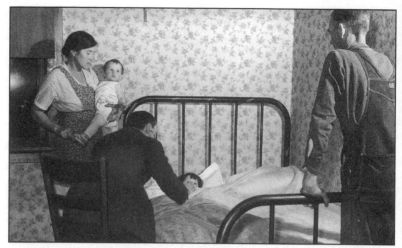

A doctor listens to the lungs of a young child. Dust pneumonia, an infection of the lungs caused by inhaling too much dirt, became a common and lethal ailment in the regions that were ravaged by dust and sand storms in the 1930s.

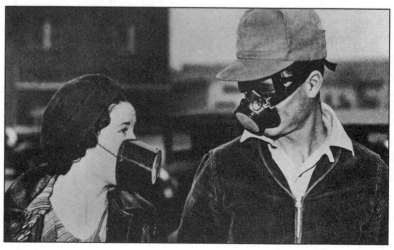

A man and woman wear masks to keep from breathing in too much of the dust that filled the air in the Dust Bowl region in 1935. As the numbers of dust pneumonia victims grew, people began wearing masks to filter the air.

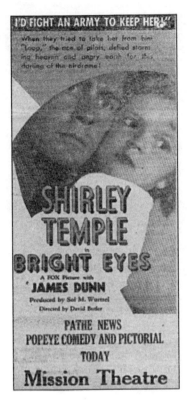

An advertisement for a movie starring the popular child star Shirley Temple, as it appeared in the Dalhart Texan *newspaper in 1935. Her films provided a temporary escape from the hardships of the Great Depression and the Dust Bowl.*

The Piggly Wiggly market posts the prices of its groceries in the Dalhart Texan *newspaper.*

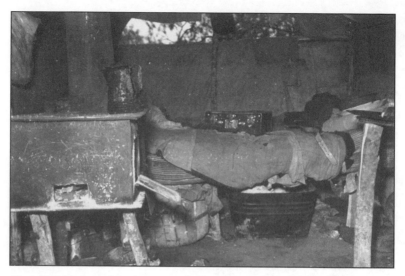

Upon arriving in California, many of the migrant families who had fled the Dust Bowl states discovered that work was hard to find. They were often so poor that they had to live in the unsanitary conditions of migrant workers' camps, where all kinds of diseases proliferated.

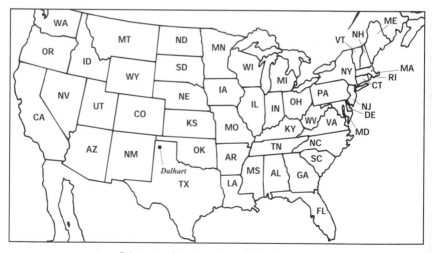

Map of the United States, highlighting Dalhart, Texas.

Acknowledgments

My heartfelt appreciation to Portia Dees and Marguerite Green, retired schoolteachers and treasured friends, who spent countless hours sharing their Dust Bowl stories and patiently answering long lists of questions; Melt White and Mary Bell Clements, who told about life in the 1930s Texas Panhandle; Nick Olson, curator of the XIT Museum in Dalhart, Texas; and Helen Bliss (Grandmother) who helped research Fort Worth historical information. Also, my friends at Scholastic: Amy Griffin, the most patient editor imaginable, whose suggestions were invaluable; Barry Denenberg, who got me off to a great start; and friend and mentor Betsy Howie.

I am especially grateful to those teachers throughout the years who have encouraged my interest in writing: Sandy Bledsoe, Sherolyn Chumley, Karen Towler, Patricia Harshey, Sharon Wilson, and principal Jack Boston. And, finally, Mum and Daddy, who've always supported me in pursuing my dreams and, most of all, in pursuing a life pleasing to Christ.

Grateful acknowledgment is made for permission to reprint the following:

Cover Portrait: CORBIS.
Cover Background: CORBIS.

Page 181 (top): Dust storm blowing into town, Photograph by Kan Elkhart, Courtesy of Hulton/Getty Collection, Negative no. MP1BW646.

Page 181 (bottom): Buried farmhouse, Arthur Rothstein/CORBIS.

Page 182 (top): Dust pneumonia, Library of Congress Prints and Photographs Division.

Page 182 (bottom): Dust masks, Brown Brothers.

Page 183 (top): Shirley Temple advertisement, The *Dalhart Texan* newspaper, Courtesy of XIT Museum, Dalhart, Texas.

Page 183 (bottom): Piggly Wiggly advertisement, The *Dalhart Texan* newspaper, Courtesy of XIT Museum, Dalhart, Texas.

Page 184 (top): Migrant camp, Photograph by Carl Mydans, Courtesy of Timepix.

Page 184 (bottom): Map by Heather Saunders.

With love for Annalee, my sister and forever friend.

About the Author

Katelan Janke, a fifteen-year-old from Dalhart, Texas, is the winner of the 1998 Arrow Book Club/Dear America Student Writing Contest. "I love history and enjoy exploring the world of my characters," says Katelan.

"The idea to write about the Dust Bowl was sparked by my town's rich past. It's an inspiration to actually live where my story takes place — I can readily imagine much of Grace Edwards's life. Often on windy, dusty days, I see a glimpse of what others survived day in and day out," she says. "I'll always treasure the time I spent visiting and interviewing Mrs. Marguerite Green and Miss Portia Dees. Even though they have lived through hardships and challenges, I admire their grateful and optimistic attitude toward life."

Katelan is a sixth-generation Texan, and, like Grace, her favorite book is *Anne of Green Gables*.

Library of Congress Cataloging-in-Publication Data
Janke, Katelan.
Survival in the storm : the dust bowl diary of Grace Edwards / by Katelan Janke.
p. cm. — (Dear America)
Summary: A twelve-year-old girl keeps a journal of her family's and friends' difficult experiences
in the Texas Panhandle, part of the "Dust Bowl," during the Great Depression. Includes a
historical note about life in America in 1935.
ISBN 0-439-21599-4
1. Depressions — 1929 — Texas — Juvenile fiction. [1. Depressions — 1929 — Texas — Fiction.
2. Dust storms — Fiction. 3. Farm life — Texas — Fiction. 4. Family life — Texas — Fiction.
5. Texas — History — 1846–1950 — Fiction. 6. Diaries — Fiction.] I. Title. II. Series.
PZ7.J24325 Su 2002
[Fic] — dc21   2002018992

10 9 8 7 6 5 4 3 2 1   02 03 04 05 06

The display type was set in Canterbury Old Style.
The text type was set in Fournier MT.
Book design by Elizabeth B. Parisi
Photo research by Dwayne Howard

Printed in the U.S.A.   23
First edition, September 2002